FLAME CROWN

Books by Kay L Moody

Truth Seer Trilogy

The Elements of Kamdaria

To receive special offers, bonus content, and info on new releases and other great reads, sign up for Kay L Moody's email list! You'll also get her short story collection for FREE.
www.KayLMoody.com/gift

Flame Crown
The Elements of Kamdaria 4
By Kay L Moody

Published by Marten Press
3731 W 10400 S, Ste 102 #205
South Jordan, UT 84009

www.MartenPress.com

Cover by Germancreative-fiverr
Edited by Deborah Spencer

ISBN: 978-17086622-2-6

The Elements of Kamdaria 4

Flame Crown

Kay L Moody

MARTEN
PRESS

ONE

ANOTHER ESCAPE WOULD BE FUN.

Talise eyed her cave-like prison cell imagining the look on her guard's face when she stole his key. Again.

Even as she pictured it, the nearby guard peered between the iron bars that locked her in. The veins in his hand pulsed as he gripped the hilt of his sword. His eyes narrowed to slits.

He seemed to know she was considering an escape. Or maybe he was naturally suspicious. In either case, she needed to throw him off.

Her fingers twitched at her sides, fighting her natural impulses. She wanted to blast a fire ball toward him, one that whizzed near enough that he could feel the heat on his cheek as it passed. She wanted to mock him for standing to the right of her cell which gave her the perfect vantage point to see the dungeon corridor and anyone who descended the staircase at its end. She wanted to point out his laughably incorrect sword stance.

But all those things would show him how powerful she really was. Though it pained her to act submissive, it also gave her freedom. When she first arrived, the spies who had kidnapped her told the others how she battled during the masquerade ball. It only took her a few days of acting weak and pathetic before the other Kessoku came to assume the spies' stories were nothing more than grossly exaggerated tales.

And right now, she needed every advantage she could get. After two weeks in a prison cell, she still had no idea what Kessoku wanted with her.

So, her actions reflected their ever-lowering opinion of her. With a whimper, she set her back against the wall. Her shoulders shivered while she brought her knees her chest and pouted. Then sniveled.

Just as she hoped, the guard rolled his eyes and turned his back on her. Now, thoughts were her only company.

Should she escape again?

If she did, it would be her second attempt. In the first attempt, she didn't expect to get far. But it did help her determine how long it took for guards to respond and how many would react. She'd also gotten a decent view of the staircase leading out of the dungeon as well as some of the rooms upstairs.

That knowledge would be invaluable for when she truly escaped. Now she had to determine if she already knew enough for the true escape, or if she needed a second fake escape to gain more knowledge of the building first?

Her knees ached the longer she hugged them to her chest. The prison cell had no bed or furniture of any kind. It merely had a pot in the corner for when nature called. Perhaps a bed would have been asking too much, but it would have been nice to be able to stand up straight in her cell.

The cave-like room had been cut from a mountain and its ceiling was slightly too short for her. When the ache in her knees became unbearable, she stretched herself out on the stone floor.

Only one spot in the cave was big enough for her to stretch out fully. She had to tuck her feet into a small indent in the stone wall, and her hair had to brush right up against the iron bars, but she fit. Barely.

At least the cave had one spot that fit her. The other prisoners brought to Kessoku's dungeons probably hadn't been able to stretch out at all.

Not that they'd been given much chance.

In the two weeks she'd spent inside the prison, six other prisoners had been carried down to the dungeons with her.

All six had been killed within hours of their arrival. After they relinquished the information Kessoku sought, they were no longer considered useful. Their executions followed immediately after.

Body odor had never been her favorite scent, but at least it masked the lingering stench of death seeping into the stone walls and floor of the dungeon.

Outside the iron bars, the Kessoku guard turned to face her again. His fingers stroked the hilt of his sword while his knees bounced. A look of eager anticipation danced in his eyes. Maybe he'd sensed how her mind whirled.

Before he could guess at her thoughts, she let out a desperate sigh and threw her head into the crook of her elbows. Her shoulders bounced up to her ears as she let out a wild sob. "I can't take this anymore. You must release me."

His hand fell away from the hilt of his sword. Shaking his head, he turned away. After only a few moments of stillness, he began tapping his toe.

The muscles in her shoulders pulled taut as she curled her body back to a sitting position. Little flutters went through her veins with each breath.

This was it.

Observation had been her only pastime for two weeks, and through it she had learned much. This particular guard always tapped his toe a few minutes before the changing of the guard.

In a split second, she made her decision. Another practice escape attempt was necessary. She knew one side of the prison corridor but not the other. Without more information, she couldn't plan a proper escape.

The shackles around her wrists turned hot while the thumping in her chest accelerated. It felt as though her heart wanted to leap from her chest and hide in that small indent of the cave where she tucked her feet at night.

Forcing another sob from her lips, she glanced toward the stairwell to the left of her cell.

Her heart quickened again, but she didn't dare fake another sob. The last one already sounded a little too hysterical.

Blink. She'd been reminding herself of the simplest things lately. *Blink or your eyes will water, and you won't see when the guard comes down the stairs.*

With a gulp, she sent another wave of fire through her wrists. The fire warmed her shackles until they glowed with heat. Without intervention, blisters would soon break out on her wrists.

Perfect.

Her shoulder scraped against the stone floor as she dragged herself toward the iron bars. "Please," she said in a pathetic sob. "I can't take another minute. Why don't you just kill me like you did the others?"

This earned her a sideways glance from the guard. She imagined the cosmetics from her eyes streaking down her cheeks along with the tears that now fell. It was nothing more than imagination, of course. After two weeks in the dungeon, the cosmetics leftover from the masquerade ball had long since faded away.

The only thing adorning her face now was a thick layer of dirt courtesy of her threadbare clothes. Still, the dirt gave something for her tears to streak through, which was sure to capture the guard's attention.

"Get back from the bars," he said through his teeth. After her last escape attempt, all the guards got jumpy when she came too close.

"I'm dying!" The chains clattered as she shook her wrists through the air. "If you want to kill me, can't you just do it quickly?"

It was a bold question, one she wouldn't have asked a week ago. But two whole weeks had passed since her capture, and they'd done nothing with her. No questions, no threats. They weren't even trying to starve her.

Even torture would have been less disconcerting than sitting in a cell day after day.

But then again, maybe that *was* the torture.

The guard pinched his nose as she neared. His curled lip reminded her she'd had nothing resembling a bath in the past two weeks.

"I said get back," he said with a snarl.

She pulled her face into a frown, but it was only half-pretend now. Apparently, he wouldn't answer her question. Not that she expected him to.

This time, he raised his hands. Sparks of flame shot from his palms in angry bursts.

He reached through the iron bars and gathered her collar in a tight fist. With sparks still bursting from his hand, he held it up to her cheek. Burning embers skipped across her skin.

The corner of his nose twitched. "My orders are to keep you alive. I don't have to keep you pretty."

An ache lanced through her throat, making it difficult to swallow. She'd nicknamed this guard "Angry" and this moment reminded her why. He liked threatening her. The singed material around her ankles proved he wasn't afraid to follow through.

Just as a flame burst from his palm, another guard finally appeared at the foot of the stairs.

Talise's wrists turned to ice a split second before she slammed her shackles against the iron bars. After heating them for so long, the sudden change in temperature, combined with the hit against iron, caused the shackles to split in half.

The guard by the stairs bolted toward her. Before he reached the cell, she'd already used air shaping to levitate the prison keys from his pocket.

His eyes widened at the sight of his keys drifting through the air. His trembling chin made his nickname—Scaredy—seem that much more appropriate.

"H-h-hey!" He had finally found his voice. "She's doing it again." His hand swatted the air as he tried to catch the keys.

They flew out of his reach not a second too soon.

Scaredy turned to the staircase and shouted even louder than before. "She's trying to escape!"

His shouts didn't cause her any anxiety. Due to her last escape attempt, she already knew what response time to expect.

However, the threatening guard—Angry—became a bigger problem with each second. He had lost his grip on her when she broke her shackles. Now, his fingers clawed at her through the bars. In one swipe, he managed to scrape off a chunk of skin from under her chin.

With one hand still shaping the keys toward her, she used the other hand to send a blast of flames at Angry's face. He ducked and caught her collar in his fist. When she finally reached for the prison keys, the shaping in her other hand stretched out in the space around her, searching for anything useful. A moment later, she shaped a clump of dirt off the cave floor.

The dirt clod slammed into Angry's neck in just the right pressure point. Even after practicing it in her head for a few days, she only half expected it to work.

To her near disbelief, Angry sank to his knees. His eyes rolled back in his head before he lost all consciousness.

Thank Kamdaria for the emperor's insistence that she learn each technique with absolute precision. Perhaps the trials had been beneficial after all.

Now it was Scaredy's turn. He dropped even faster than Angry.

She didn't dare kill either of them. Even though they kept her alive so far, if she killed any guards, they'd probably kill her in return. And there were too many of them for her to fight on her own. Her best chance was to run.

The lock on her cell door clicked open a moment later. Talise wrapped the key tight in her palm and rushed down the corridor to the doorway on the right side of the dungeon.

Now to see how far she could get.

TWO

THE DUNGEON CORRIDOR BENT INTO A curve, which perfectly obscured Talise from view once she rounded it.

Her eyes darted left and right while her feet propelled her forward. The narrow corridor could fit no more than two people running side by side. Still, two was one more than her.

More information bombarded her with each step. Splotches of dirt covered the gray walls. Creating a similar look would be impossible.

One of her escape ideas hinged on disguising herself with dirt and rocks to blend in with the walls. That idea was officially out. Even if she somehow mastered the necessary artistry of disguise, the corridor didn't have enough room to avoid being trampled by oncoming guards.

Weapons clattered together as backup finally trampled down the staircase. The Kessoku barked orders at each other as they went. If she counted their voices correctly, a small squad of six or seven hustled after her. Just like last time.

Based on her timing, she still had half a minute before she'd be in their view. Her eyes drifted upward. Could something up there be useful?

To her surprise, a small alcove sat in the ceiling. She could probably fit inside it perfectly, which would have been a genius way to hide from the guards. If only she could think of a way up there.

But her time had run out.

The guards barreled forward, which meant she had to barrel forward too. Her feet winced with each step. Not for the first time, she cursed herself for removing her shoes during that fight at the masquerade ball. On the next footfall, the ball of her foot landed squarely on a sharp rock. Her knee flew up to her chest on instinct while she let out a sharp cry of pain.

They had taken away her gown when she first arrived in the dungeon and given her an itchy burlap tunic and pants to wear. They never made any attempt to supply her with footwear.

Hissing at her bare feet, she ran again. This corridor went on longer than she expected. Even with Kessoku close behind her, she'd had time to find numerous openings in the ceiling, though none of them seemed to lead anywhere in particular. They were more like vents.

But for what?

The answer became clear a moment later. A cloud of black smoke billowed out of a hole in the ground. The smoke slithered across the ceiling until it found the nearby vents.

A sudden giddiness took hold inside her when she looked at the hole again.

An opening.

She rushed toward it without a thought. Smoke meant fire. She knew that. This was probably some sort of chimney with burning flames at the bottom. Dangerous, but was it really that dangerous for her?

She could shape ice inside her body. Kessoku would never think to secure an opening that led to flames because who could possibly walk through fire and live?

As the only ice shaper in history, she might be the only one.

The guards shouted as she lowered herself down the opening. Her feet quickly found footholds, which brought her out of their grasp just in time.

The tip of a sword brushed across her fingertips as she lowered herself again. Her other foot found a foothold much faster than she expected. She eyed the chimney as she lowered herself down a third time.

Several smoothed-out indents adorned the inside of the chimney wall. They worked perfectly as foot and handholds, but why would they be inside a chimney? Perhaps the Kessoku had once used this tunnel as a ladder before it became a chimney.

Black smoke filled her lungs as she drew in a breath. If only she'd had time to wrap a piece of cloth over her nose and mouth. A hacking cough escaped her lips. That's when the jeers began.

"Enjoy being cooked alive," one guard shouted down at her.

"Hope you don't lose your grip from all the sweat." This earned a round of raucous laughter from the other guards.

The drips of sweat sliding down her chin *had* been worrying her. But they didn't need to know that.

For a moment, she brushed the fear aside and imagined what she'd see at the bottom. She hoped to find a tiny kitchen with a wizened old cook who wouldn't know what to do when a dirty girl emerged from the chimney. It was unlikely, but that didn't stop her from hoping.

Kessoku's whole base, at least from what she'd seen, had been cut from a mountain side. Since the highest mountains in Kamdaria were in the

Crown, she guessed this base was also in the Crown.

Either the emperor had been wrong about Kessoku's base being in the Gate, or—more likely—this wasn't Kessoku's main base at all.

That thought both excited and terrified her. If this *was* Kessoku's main base, then all the prisoners they took months ago, including Wendy's brother, Cyrus, were surely dead. But if this was only one of many bases, Cyrus might still be alive. But it also meant Kessoku was an even bigger threat than they thought.

More jeers bounced off the walls of the chimney while she found another foothold. Her hacking coughs came out faster now. She had already shaped ice into her skin to help fend off some of the heat.

The jeering grew louder.

"See you soon, Princess. It won't be long before you realize there is no escape."

The words felt like lead on her shoulders. She wanted to ignore them, but the rising temperature made it impossible. Each time she lowered herself down the chimney, the heat seeped through her skin, melting away the ice in her skin. The smoke coated her throat and burned her eyes.

She tried using air to shape away the black smoke, but more would replace it almost immediately. Even with ice shaping, the temperature in her body surged to dangerous heights.

After lowering herself down to the next foothold, she understood why the heat swelled with such intensity.

Her dream of a small kitchen fire cooking a pot of stew was far from the reality before her. The flames licking the bottom edges of the chimney burned as high as a bonfire. Higher.

Below her was an incinerator.

It didn't matter. That's what she wanted to tell herself.

She was the first ice shaper in all of Kamdaria. That had to mean something.

She lowered herself again, and it felt like someone had poured hot water down her back. It took a moment to realize, the water came from her own sweat. Heat roared inside her. She couldn't tell what was heat and was ice. The sensations blended into one stabbing stream under her skin.

Her foot hovered over the next foothold. She sent another blast of ice through her, but it felt more like fire. Her head hung as the truth settled like a rock in her gut.

Even with ice shaping, she'd never survive a fire that big.

Not to mention her lungs constricted from all the smoke inside them. Tears blurred her vision also thanks to the stinging black smoke. This was over now.

From above, she could just made out the roaring laughter of the guards.

"Give up yet? We have a nice cell for you up here."

Their laughter turned riotous. They must have seen how her progress had halted. They must have known she'd be climbing back soon.

Her heart sank, taking up residence where her stomach should have been. Had she gotten enough information? She knew the layout of the dungeon perfectly now. She'd found a few hiding spots. She knew where *not* to hide. She knew how fast the guards would come and how many there would be. Was it enough? Did she know enough to actually escape next time?

Clutching the prison key in her palm, she began the slow ascent up the chimney.

It had to be enough. She'd survived twelve years since Kessoku first tried to kill her. She wasn't about to let them succeed now.

THE GUARD'S TAUNTING became gleeful as Talise neared the top of the chimney. She still held the prison key tight in her hand. They'd take it back soon enough. Before they did, she let the sweat gather in her palm until she had enough water to shape over the entire key.

Moving water over the key helped her memorize the shape of it. The corners and rivets and curves all became familiar as she shaped the water into ice and back to water again.

The water gently flowed over the key as she climbed. Freezing and unfreezing the water allowed her to engrain its shape into her memory. Her mind wandered over the dimensions of it as she committed its every curve to memory.

The guards would steal the key as soon as she reached the top. Since she had now attempted twice to escape, she wasn't likely to ever be near the key again. They'd take even greater precautions to keep it out of her reach.

But if she could memorize its shape, she could make her own key with ice. As long as she got it cold enough, the ice key would work to unlock her cell.

The guards continued to laugh as she crawled out the chimney and onto the stone floor of the dungeon corridor. They didn't bother being gentle as they slapped a new pair of shackles onto her wrists.

She immediately fell back into her frightened princess routine. It wouldn't be as convincing with her recent escape, but that wouldn't stop her from trying.

Wiping a line through the soot on her arm, she let out a sob. "Can't I have some water to wash myself?"

Her shoulders shook with a shiver as she raised her arm up to her nose. No imagination was required to bring a look of disgust over her face. Even in the Storm, she had never smelled so bad.

The nearest guard held the chains between her shackles as he tore the key from her grip. "You think we'd give you water just so you could shape ice daggers or something at us? Think again, Princess."

Ice daggers.

Now *that* would have been fun. Sadly, they kept all water out of her reach, except just enough to keep her alive. As tempting as it had been to use that water for shaping, she needed it for drinking. She did have a fair amount of sweat still dripping down her skin. Perhaps that would give her the water she needed for the ice key.

To keep up her act, she scowled at the nearest guard and threw her nose in the air. "You all deserve to rot for how you're treating me. Why don't you just kill me?"

She hoped with half a dozen guards around, at least one of them would be stupid enough to answer. People tended to lose their heads in a crowd.

Luckily, one guard seemed delighted in her capture just enough to forget about holding his tongue. "There's someone you have to meet first, Princess. He has questions for you."

They all got some sort of sick pleasure from calling her *princess*. It roiled her insides every time. Regardless, she had gotten the answer she wanted. If someone had questions for her, then Kessoku wanted information. That was good. It put her in a position of power.

The loose-lipped guard had been jabbed by the four guards nearest to him. His feet shuffled forward as his ears turned bright red. He clamped his mouth shut and dropped his eyes to the ground.

When they arrived back at her prison cell, the threatening guard, Angry, stood. Apparently, he had regained consciousness. His jaw clenched as he beckoned Talise back inside her cell. "Welcome back, Princess." A smirk curled his lips up, and he made a sweeping mock bow. "I have a surprise for you."

Her shoulders shuddered as another guard locked the iron door, sealing her in once again.

Angry moved his hands in a small circle while he shaped a ring of fire between his palms. Soon, his flame took the shape of a crown.

The design was crude. Nothing like Aaden's magnificent cherry blossom trees. But it didn't matter. The implication was clear.

He had threatened to burn her earlier and hadn't been given the pleasure. He wouldn't be denied it a second time. His face screwed up as he levitated the crown toward her.

Though she had played the frightened princess since she arrived, her chin trembled with genuine fear. Her feet stumbled backward as her mind whirled.

Sweat. She still had plenty of sweat on her back and arms. Now it was time to use it.

Her hands fell to her sides as she shaped the water away from her body and into a water ball behind her back. She tried shaping water out of the air as well, but the dry heat of the dungeon wouldn't allow for it.

Moving her fingers as little as possible, she levitated the water ball up to her head. Once there, she shaped it into a thin layer that could rest just above her hair. She barely had a single moment to freeze the water before the flame crown landed on her hair.

The ice protected her, but she couldn't let the guards know that. With a firm hold on the ice shaping, Talise collapsed to her knees and let out a wail.

Her shoulders shook and her body shivered as the seconds crawled forward. Wincing and groaning were the only actions she could manage without losing a grip on her ice shaping. Still, it seemed to be working. One of the guards scratched his neck. Another looked away.

"Stop it!" Her screams reverberated through the dungeon walls, each more desperate than the last. The flames had melted through most of the ice now, so her performance really had to count. She clawed at her own face, letting her body shiver as her eyes rolled back in their sockets.

"Please," she said through a sob.

Scaredy, who had also regained consciousness, touched Angry on the arm. "That's enough, Flint. We need to keep her alive."

It surprised her that Angry would have a name as common as Flint. Even more surprising was the softness in Scaredy's eyes. He pretended to be unbothered by her pain, that he cared only for their orders to keep her alive. Yet, distress drifted through his eyes when he glanced through the iron bars of her cell. Perhaps her cries had reminded him of his humanity.

The moment Flint shaped the flame crown away, Talise threw herself to the stone floor in a fit of sobs. She bunched up her hair and let out unintelligible words that almost sounded like "hair" and "ruined" and "singed."

Luckily, the guards were too certain of their success to investigate. With any luck, they'd never notice that her hair was as thick and long as always, except for a few burnt strands. The ice she had used to protect her head had all turned to steam now, but at least it had protected her when she needed it.

She could rest easier now.

If someone was coming to see her, they weren't going to kill her. At least not yet.

That gave her just enough time to gather the water she needed for an ice key. In the meantime, she'd continue to observe their routines and learn as much as possible for her true escape.

No matter what, her third one would be successful. Hopefully she could get out before her mysterious visitor arrived.

THREE

THE GUARDS WERE GETTING NERVOUS.

Talise had been in the dungeon for three weeks now, and the signs were easy to spot. Each changing of the guard came with tense whispers. Sometimes two would come down the stairs: one for watching her, the other for changing out the guard.

Despite her weak princess routine, they seemed to know she had plans brewing. And of course, they were right. She'd spent the last week gathering water for her escape. To her dismay, it took longer than she expected.

The dungeon air was dry, probably because of the nearby chimney. The dry heat made it difficult to shape water out of the air.

Her solution had been to keep small bits of water each time they gave her a drink. By taking a tiny bit each time, her stash had almost grown large enough for the ice key.

Since her visitor hadn't yet arrived, she took her time to make sure the water she had would be enough.

The guard in front of her cell started pacing. He did that a lot. So much, in fact, it had earned him the nickname Pacey. He kept throwing suspicious glances at her. It seemed like a good time to play the pathetic princess.

She pulled her knees up to her chest and let her head hang. Small whimpers escaped her next. When he still wouldn't stop staring, she went a step further. "I just want to go home," she said through a whimper.

Pacey rolled his eyes before turning away.

Once he turned, she rolled her eyes right back. Were they really convinced by her act so easily? Or maybe they didn't know her whole history. She had survived the Storm, after all. This was nothing in comparison.

With the guard's back to her, thinking became easier. She kept whimpering, but her mind wandered back to the night of the masquerade ball. When she first woke up in Kessoku's dungeon, she had thought Aaden would be there with her. But he wasn't. Without seeing or hearing anything about him in her three weeks there, she assumed the Kessoku spies had left him unconscious back at the palace.

While rocking herself back and forth on the stone floor, every other event from the night of her kidnapping played through her head. Just like it had a dozen other times.

One of her guards, Tempest, told them about Kessoku spies. Then, Commander Blaise told them to do nothing. Next, her friends found out her true identity while they were in the treasury. Then, they fought Kessoku in the ballroom.

Her heart always started beating faster when she remembered the rest of the night. Aaden's questions.

His kiss.

Everything played through her mind as she clung to the same question that had been with her since that night.

Who had betrayed her?

Kessoku *did* have someone working in the palace. She knew that for sure. The Kessoku spies had targeted her soldiers even when they wore masquerade clothes in a crowded ballroom. Plus, the spies had escaped after being taken to the dungeons. They couldn't have done it without help.

But did it have to be one of her friends?

Kessoku stole the family tree *before* she and her friends made it to the treasury. It had her name right on it.

Yes, it would have been a stretch for Kessoku to assume it was her by the name alone, but there were other clues. She was the right age. She was from the Storm but could shape anyway. She knew the palace better than she should have, though she didn't think anyone had noticed that.

They could have guessed it on their own. They could have figured it out.

Or, maybe one of the emperor's guards had let the secret out. The emperor had chosen his trusted guards based on loyalty. They all seemed eager to die a thousand deaths before they'd betray Kamdaria. So, it probably wasn't one of them either.

But maybe they had let the secret out unintentionally.

Maybe they said something in passing to a kitchen servant and the servant had repeated it to just the right person. Something that wouldn't have been incriminating on its own, but to someone who had other pieces of the puzzle...

Anyone could have given the secret away. Hundreds of people lived on the palace grounds. And it had been twelve years. Just because the secret got out, didn't mean it was one of her friends.

Talise hugged her knees tighter to her chest, surprised that her whimpering wasn't all pretend now.

Aaden.

That's who she really feared. Wendy and Claye she had known for years, but Aaden only a few months. And he always had an air of mystery about him. And why had he been so interested in her anyway? What did she have to offer? Did he only want her for information?

As soon as the thoughts came, they turned around again. It couldn't be Aaden. It *couldn't* be.

Yes, he would have had ample time during the fight in the ballroom to share her secret with the spies. And afterward when she had spent all that time dressing wounds and checking on her soldiers, he could have snuck off to help the Kessoku spies escape.

But what about his face when they'd kidnapped her?

She remembered clearly how her name came out of his mouth in a strangled cry. She remembered how he struggled against his own captors, desperate to get to her.

He never looked smug or relieved that Kessoku was there.

He looked surprised. Desperate.

Afraid.

He had tried to save her.

And what about the kiss?

It had occurred to her more than once that maybe the kiss was a ruse. Maybe he did it to distract her, so she wouldn't hear when Kessoku entered the room.

But it didn't feel like a ruse.

It felt passionate and raw. Nothing had felt more real in her entire life.

She had appealed to logic several times since getting captured. The simple truth was she couldn't know for sure if Aaden was involved with Kessoku. He *could* have betrayed her. He'd had time. He'd had opportunity. But there were just as many evidences he wasn't involved. Her brain couldn't tell her whether it was safe to trust him.

So, instead, she trusted her heart.

It wasn't Aaden. She didn't *know* it, but she could *feel* it.

The guard began pacing again. The torch flickered in its hanging on the wall. Being down in the dungeon with no light from the outside made it difficult to tell time. After her time there, she had picked up on several clues.

Twice a day, someone brought a new torch down and retrieved the old one. Morning and night, she had discovered. During the day, the guards looked more alert. At night, they looked more somber.

Plus, during the day, she could hear a smattering of voices coming from up the stairs. The voices were always loudest at mealtimes.

The noises were picking up now. Breakfast. Once everyone upstairs finished eating, they'd bring the leftovers down to her. Whoever guarded her got to eat off the plate first. Getting leftovers usually meant she received little more than burnt pieces of bread and tough meat. Sometimes small bits of bruised fruit sat on the plate.

None of it bothered her, though she always pretended to be disgusted by it. Of all the foolish things Kessoku did, feeding her was the stupidest of all. It kept her strength up. Ready for her true escape.

TALISE CURLED HERSELF into a ball. Her cheek rested on the cool stone floor while heavy tears dripped from her eyes. It was dangerous to cry. Each tear brought her closer to dehydration. But it also gave her more water to collect for the ice key, so the risk was worth it.

Occasionally, she'd use one arm to pull her knees closer, just so she could wipe her tears on the burlap fabric of her pants. It would be easier to collect the water that way.

Her smell was getting out of control.

The guard stared her down as she trembled on the stone floor. She had nicknamed this guard Beady because of her small black eyes.

Beady never seemed as convinced by Talise's act as the other guards. Then again, she had every right to be suspicious since the entire thing was fake.

But, even if this guard knew to be cautious, it didn't make her smart enough to realize only one of Talise's arms was visible.

The other arm she had hidden behind her back while she continually shaped her little ball of water. With her fingers pressing through the air, she shaped the water into an exact replica of the prison key.

Once she had frozen it for a few moments, she would melt it and start the whole process over again. Each time, she imagined the key in her mind, tracing over each turn and edge. For the key to work, she had to get the shape exactly right.

Soft footsteps sounded down the corridor, coming from the staircase to the left. Beady immediately jumped to attention. She was at the bottom of the staircase in three steps.

Talise knew whose face to expect before it appeared. She had memorized the sound of all their footsteps during her imprisonment. The boy who brought her water had a round face with friendly eyes. He seemed more distressed by her capture than the others, but maybe her smell bothered him more than anything.

Beady frowned at the sight of the boy. Had she been expecting someone else? Her shoulders dropped as she gestured toward Talise. "Go on. Get it over with."

The boy wore the same brown burlap as Talise, which suggested he was also a prisoner in some way. But maybe not. His burlap wasn't as stiff as hers. It looked well-worn from lots of washing. He carried a wooden bucket with a wooden ladle.

The guards got water eight times a day and four times during the night. They allowed Talise half that amount. When her water came, the bucket was merely for show. Not even a ladle's worth of water sat in the bottom.

Talise froze her levitating ball of water and tucked the ice ball into her pocket. Smacking her lips, she crept toward the iron bars.

"Hey!" shouted Beady. "You know the rules. Stay more than an arm's length away from the bars."

Talise nodded as she stepped back. She wanted to roll her eyes. As if she'd be stupid enough to attack anyone from inside her cell. Something like that was sure to be a death sentence. Instead, she kept smacking her lips and eyed the wooden bucket greedily, trying to look as pathetic as ever.

When the boy stepped up to the bars, Talise curled her hands into fists and held them tight at her sides. Just like she was supposed to do.

Now, Beady shaped the remaining water out of the bucket and levitated it toward Talise. As always, Talise smacked her lips as she drank from the levitating ball of water. This caused great dribbles of water to slide down her chin.

Once the boy left and Beady turned away, Talise would collect the extra water and add it to the frozen ball in her pocket.

Soon, the boy left. She didn't have long to collect the water before another pair of footsteps sounded from the staircase. This pair of feet sounded different from her regular guards. Beady rushed to the foot of the stairs where a man wearing black stood.

"Is he here yet?" Beady whispered.

The sound of Beady's voice carried through the dungeon, but Talise had to strain to hear the response.

"He's just putting his horse in the stables," the man replied. "He'll be down in a minute."

Beady turned back to look at Talise with a nasty grin.

So, Talise's visitor had arrived. She had hoped for a few more days to prepare for her escape.

Still, as long as she didn't give anything away to her visitor, she still had a little time.

Not wanting to appear like she'd heard anything, Talise sniffled and sat against the back wall of her cell with a frown. She tucked the ice ball into the small indent where she put her feet at night. Then, she rocked herself back and forth, trying to look weak and scared.

It didn't take long before heavy footsteps came tromping down the stairs. These were definitely unrecognizable from any of the feet she knew.

A tall man with broad shoulders appeared at the bottom of the stairs a few moments later. A gasp escaped Talise's lips before she could stop it.

"General," Beady said with a short bow.

He nodded in return and moved down the corridor. He carried a small red stool and puffed his chest out as he strode toward her. Over his heart, he worse Kessoku's symbol of three interlocking circles. Not just a member of Kessoku, but a high ranking one.

Talise's heart seemed to have forgotten how to beat. The man set his stool directly in front of her cell, and he dared to smile as he settled into the seat.

Of all the things she expected her visitor to look like, *this* was not what she imagined. Not this at all.

The man wore a goatee. It must have been a family tradition.

His brown eyes shined bright. Even in the torch light, she could make out small orange flecks around his irises. A few gray strands peppered his neatly combed hair. When he smiled, his lips curved into a look so familiar, it made her stomach churn with horror.

The resemblance was uncanny. While Aaden only looked vaguely like his grandfather, *this* man was practically his mirror image. The only difference was his advancement in age. Even with no introduction, Talise knew exactly whom she was staring at.

Lucian Sato.

Aaden's father.

FOUR

EVERY LIMB IN TALISE'S BODY HAD frozen. Her brain kept telling her to play stupid. To act weak. But her brain couldn't overpower the thumping organ in her chest.

The only movements she made now were the automatic ones. Breathing. Blinking.

Everything else had gone still.

"Talise," Lucian said with a nod. Her gut twisted, causing a shot of bile to dance up her throat. "You're much older than last time I saw you."

How dare he? Her stomach churned again. How dare he say her name so casually? And reference that he knew her as a child?

One part of her ached to clutch her stomach, anything to ease the churning inside it. Another part of her wanted to blast fire balls in his face regardless of the consequences. And the last part? It wanted to give up right there on the stone floor. It wanted her to collapse and never get back up again.

What had Aaden said to Claye during the masquerade ball? "My father was idiotic but not treasonous."

But here Lucian sat with three interlocking circles adorning his chest. Had Aaden known all along? Was he a part of the charade?

Lucian cleared his throat. "I'm sure I'm the last person you expected to see today—"

"I have no idea who you are." Talise cut him off, then tossed her head back with her best impression of boredom. Her brain had finally caught up to the moment. Apparently, she had decided to play a disinterested spoiled brat.

Lucian had no reaction to her act. He merely nodded. "Ah, forgive me. I have worked hard to keep my involvement with Kessoku a secret, for my family's sake. But I've been a member since the beginning. My name is Lucian Sato." His head tilted toward the bars as he raised his eyebrows. "I'm sure you know me now, don't you?"

Talise pressed her back into the stone wall behind her. Every trace of the disinterested brat fell away from her face. Feigned ignorance would be no help to her now. He knew who she was, and he knew she'd know the name *Sato*.

With her lips pressed into a tight line, she blinked back at him. She wouldn't give him the satisfaction of answering his question.

Silence was her only power now.

Lucian nodded. He understood her perfectly, and the nod seemed like his feeble attempt to gain back some control.

"Have you seen Emperor Kamdar's gravestone?" he asked.

The word *yes* very nearly popped out of Talise's mouth without her permission. The question took her off guard so completely, answering it almost seemed like the best option. She *had* seen Kamdar's gravestone before. Only once and it had been many years ago. The stone was so weathered, the markings in the gravestone were only barely visible.

Other than the faded markings, she couldn't remember anything significant about the gravestone. Had its location been secret? She didn't remember that, but then again, she had been four years old when she saw it.

What could Kessoku possibly want with it? Her confusion only led to fear. If she didn't know what information he sought, anything she said could give it away.

"Have you seen it?" Lucian asked again.

Her lips remained pressed shut. The disinterested brat didn't seem like such a stretch of the imagination now. What did she care about Kamdar's gravestone?

Lucian seemed intent to learn more, but she had more important things to consider. All the things she knew for sure. First, Kessoku had someone in the palace who worked for them. Second, Aaden's father was a member of Kessoku, which made Aaden the most likely spy. Third, Aaden wasn't the spy.

Maybe that last one she didn't know for sure, but it felt like the truth. She had seen Aaden's face when they all realized she was the princess. He had been just as surprised as the others. Maybe even more so.

And what about when he yelled at Claye for suggesting Kessoku might recruit him? Or any time he talked about his father? His father had ruined his life. He had shown genuine emotion. Genuine heartbreak.

He couldn't have known how deeply involved with Kessoku his father was. And he certainly couldn't be involved himself.

Maybe the whole thing was an act. Maybe Aaden had been lying from the moment he met her, but he didn't seem capable of that kind of deception.

When he was angry, she knew he was angry. When he wanted to kiss her, he made it clear in every part of his body language.

He *couldn't* have lied to her like that.

Which meant he had to have been as ignorant of his father's involvement as she was.

Lucian sighed. He seemed to understand all at once that she wouldn't answer any of his questions. "Do you know what Kessoku means?"

Again, his question took her off guard. As he spoke, Lucian traced his finger over each of the three interlocking circles on his tunic. "Kessoku means unity. Our mission is to destroy the division between the three rings of Kamdaria. We want all people to have equal opportunity, equal punishment. Equal livelihood."

Talise blinked.

Her enemy wanted the same things she did? Was that even possible?

Her mind whirled with a thousand possibilities. Maybe they could work together. Maybe they could fight the same cause. It was slightly inconvenient they wanted to kill her because otherwise...

In a flash, the truth came back to her like a crushing avalanche. They'd killed her entire family all those years ago. Not humanely.

And not just the royal family either. They'd murdered servants, guards, court members,

Talise's friends. And what about their attack during the masquerade ball? They hadn't killed anyone that night, but not for lack of trying.

She felt her stare harden. It didn't matter what Kessoku wanted to achieve. She'd never approve of their methods.

"You see...," Lucian said, stroking his goatee.

Talise gulped, forcing her eyes away from his. The movement reminded her so much of Aaden. He always stroked his goatee when thinking. Lucian's eyes reminded her of Aaden too. Everything about it felt wrong.

Lucian continued. "What we fight for is a good thing. You lived in the Storm. I'm sure you've doubted the need for a division of classes."

She gritted her teeth. So, they did know about her living in the Storm. What else did they know?

For a moment, Lucian's eyes flicked toward the staircase. It was only then that Talise noticed Beady, her guard from earlier, disappear up the stairs.

Lucian's voice raised slightly, as if making sure Beady could still hear him though she headed up the stairs. "We have important work to do."

The intentional way he spoke brought Talise's attention forward. While her mind tried to work out what it could mean, Lucian stood. He wrapped a hand around one of the iron bars. His eyes turned tender.

"Please," he said in a brand-new voice. This one felt soft like worn leather. "I have a personal request."

Just like every new development during this interrogation, this one took her off-guard. Her eyes darted around her cell and back to Lucian. If his game was to confuse her, he played it well.

Yet, nothing about his eyes spoke of strategy. Like he said, it looked personal.

"I have devoted my life to Kessoku, which I don't regret, but it did require some sacrifices. I wanted to ask you about my son, Aaden. You've seen him? How is he?"

The words stabbed her in the gut. When she played them over in her mind, they stabbed her again in the heart.

How *is* he? Was he seriously asking after his son? The person whose life he had destroyed? And what about her own family? Considering his position, she couldn't believe the gall of him to ask such a request.

She had never been able to hate Lucian because his mistake had supposedly been an accident. He had tricked everyone with his act as a fool. Even the emperor never dreamed Lucian had been involved with Kessoku.

But now he stood here, and she finally knew the truth. For the first time in her life, she allowed the hate to flow through her freely.

Lucian didn't seem to notice how tight she had clenched her jaw. He didn't seem to hear the heavy puffs escaping her nostrils. The white-knuckled fists at her side? They seemed to be nothing to him. He was lost in his own world.

"I know he's a Master Shaper now." The pride in his eyes sparkled, which only gave her the strong desire to hurl fire balls at his face. "I can't get many reports about him, for his own safety. But I haven't seen him in many years. Is he tall like me? Or shorter like his grandfather? Does he still whistle when he's nervous? Does he stroke his goatee when he's thinking? Does he have one? I'm assuming he has one."

It took everything in her just to breathe. The questions came fast, and each one made her lose another ounce of control. She wanted to scream at him. Wanted to burn him. Knowing she'd probably be killed for either of those things, she managed to force her emotions down.

The best she could do was steer the conversation the way she wanted it to go. But she'd stick to the facts. The things Lucian already knew.

She parted her lips just enough to let words out. "Wasn't he supposed to live in the Storm? I thought he had a black *X* on his ID card. Because of you." She couldn't help adding that last part.

"I would have rescued him from the Storm." He said the words in a matter-of-fact tone, but a trace of guilt still lingered through them.

"That's..." *Impossible*. That's what she was about to say. Nobody could be rescued from the Storm. ID cards were checked at every gate between the rings. Special passes were required to travel between the rings. It had taken Marmie months to get the pass for Talise's academy testing.

Yet, he spoke with such certainty. Did he have a way to rescue people from the Storm? Had he done it before? She managed to ask, "How?"

But Lucian had moved on. Apparently, he didn't realize what he just admitted to. That was something she could use later, hopefully.

"It's better he's a Master Shaper. He can stay with his grandparents that way. What is he like? Tell me anything." Lucian stared through the bars with hope in his eyes.

Thoughts raced through her mind. She wanted to scream at him. *He has a scar across his left eye because of your soldiers!* More than anything, she wanted to scar his face with fire.

But the true power of her silence took hold. With her best imitation of Aaden, Talise smirked back at Lucian.

She could tell him many things about his son. All the things he wanted to hear and more. She knew him better than almost anyone.

With her smirk, she made sure Lucian understood how much she knew. And how much she wouldn't say.

The sparkle in his eyes darkened. His grip on the iron bar clenched. He had never seemed particularly kind, but all trace of friendliness vanished from his features. A cruel smile overtook his face. When he spoke again, his words were careful. Precise.

"It's a shame you're the princess. We thought you could be an ally when we first heard about you. A Master Shaper from the Storm? It seemed too good to be true."

He shrugged his shoulders as he settled back into his stool. His demeanor darkened with each word. "But Kamdaria is too ruined now. A simple change won't be a real change at all. For anything to get better we must completely overthrow the government. We must start over. There's no other way."

He glanced at her through narrowed eyes. "It's nothing personal, but we are going to kill you. You know that, don't you?"

He was trying to scare her. The way he curled his lips. The way he spoke the words with casual indifference. The way he made her feel like the tablet on a Forces board instead of a person. His life was nothing to her.

It *did* scare her.

Down to her core, the fear shook through her. But when it came time to react, she merely crossed her arms in front of her chest. With her earlier smirk still growing, she said, "Good luck."

She didn't know what possessed her to say such a thing. She'd probably regret it. A lot. And very soon. But as she sat back against the stone, she added with a touch of laughter, "You'll need it."

The cold, calculated look of Lucian's face fell away. Apparently, she had shocked him out of whatever game he thought he could play. He seemed to recognize mind tricks would get him nowhere. He seemed ready to try a direct approach.

He sat still on his stool. His voice cold, no emotion coloring it. "Have you seen Emperor Kamdar's gravestone?"

Silence had been her power, but this time, one word would give her even more. She looked him square in the eye and said, "Yes."

"Are there markings on it?" he asked.

Silence.

He narrowed his eyes. "Does the grave have a circle with four markings inside?"

Silence.

"It's the same as the symbol for Master Shapers. A circle divided into four sections. In the top section is a waterfall, the right section has a tornado, the bottom section has a tree, and the left section has a flame."

Silence.

He slammed a fist against the iron bars. "I know you know what I'm talking about. Is the Master Shaper symbol on his gravestone? Is it part of the stone or is it carved into a metal piece that's attached to the gravestone?"

The stream of questions came so fast, she couldn't help but react to the last one. One eye twitched. A memory had been triggered inside her. One so deep, she couldn't remember who had been there or what they'd been saying. All she remembered was the word *amulet*.

The memory frayed, slipping away. But then she snatched onto it again when she remembered Marmie had been there. The edges of her memory sharpened into focus. Marmie had been talking to a maid. They were trying to keep the amulet secret, but from who, Talise had never known.

"It's probably about this big," Lucian said, forming a circle with his thumb and pointer finger. "And the metal is probably thin like a pendant, but if it's attached to the gravestone, you wouldn't know that for sure."

That *sounded* like an amulet. Memories tugged at her from every corner. Had that been what Marmie wanted kept secret? Kamdar's amulet?

When Talise came back to the present moment, Lucian grinned at her. In a rumbling voice, he asked, "Where is the gravestone?"

She had given away too much. Even without speaking, she had revealed more than she intended. Now Lucian knew she had heard of the amulet. He also seemed to assume the amulet was a part of Kamdar's gravestone.

It wasn't. At least not as far as she remembered, but she wasn't about to correct his assumption. And even if the amulet wasn't on the gravestone, it could have been nearby.

He glared.

Her stomach roiled inside. How could she stop herself from divulging secrets when she didn't even speak a word? She decided to answer all his questions from now on. She just wouldn't answer them the way he wanted.

"Where?" he asked again.

A laugh danced from her lips. "If you're just going to kill me, why would I tell you anything?"

With the snap of his fingers, Talise's earlier guard appeared at the bottom of the stairs.

"Starve her," Lucian said. "Once she loses her shaping from malnourishment, she should be more cooperative. Relay my order to the kitchens."

The guard nodded and disappeared up the stairs.

Talise wanted to hold her breath but she forced a steady stream of air in and out of her mouth. Now they'd gotten smart. Malnourishment was a painful way to die. An effective form of torture. If she lost her shaping, she'd probably do anything for food.

Too bad for him. She wouldn't be there long enough for any of that to happen.

She'd escape tonight. Hopefully she had enough water now. She'd leave in between the second and third changing of the guard. When the guards were the most tired and the Kessoku's base was the quietest.

Lucian stared at her. The anger that flashed in his eyes only a moment earlier had faded away. Again, his face softened. "If you tell me about my son, I'll make sure you get a little bread each day. I just want to know, is he happy?"

Happy?

The words were like a punch to the gut. This man had killed her entire family. He had probably helped plan the recent attacks on the palace. He seemed to have no guilt for murdering as long as it fit his agenda.

But none of those crimes mattered to her now. What mattered was Aaden. This man had taken everything away from his son. He never even apologized. He did nothing when Aaden's grandparents took him away. Didn't try to protest.

He destroyed Aaden's life without a single glance back. And now he had the audacity to *care* what had happened to him?

Talise decided she would rather stab herself with an ice dagger than tell Lucian anything about his son.

She gritted her teeth together. Her words were fire. "Rot. In. Flames."

FIVE

BENEATH TALISE'S CHEEK, THE STONE floor shook enough to wake her from a fitful sleep. Her hand went straight for the ice ball.

Still safe in her pocket.

She shaped the water that had melted into the burlap and refroze it into the ice ball. And then she could breathe again.

A little more sleep would have been useful. She needed to be at her best for her escape attempt that night. But the shaking concerned her.

Letting out a long yawn, she turned to assess the dungeon.

Her latest guard wasn't even watching her. She stood at the foot of the stairs clutching a sword. Ready for battle.

In an instant, Talise leaned forward. This was new. Did it have anything to do with the shaking stone?

Two other guards whispered with the guard that was supposed to be watching her. They also carried swords.

Talise wanted to sit up. Wanted to lean closer. But she also didn't want her captors to think she noticed how tension thickened the air.

She settled on scooting closer to the bars of her cell while idly stretching and scratching various parts of her body.

Even though they spoke in whispers, she still picked out a few words of the guards' conversation. Most of the conversation made no sense, but one phrase stuck out to her. "General is safe, left earlier."

Talise's ears pricked with attention.

The female guard whipped around and snarled at Talise before more of their conversation could be heard. The guard looked ready to deliver a death blow.

This seemed the perfect moment to appear ignorant. And weak.

Talise gave out a long stretch before she curled back against the cave wall of her cell. After smacking her lips, she pouted, trying to look as pathetic as she could. "I'm so thirsty. Isn't it time for water yet?"

Now all three of the guards snarled.

"We're starving you, remember?" the female guard said with a snap.

Hugging her knees to her chest, Talise let out a whimper. "Even water?"

"Shut up!" the guard shouted in response. She turned to the other two guards who both stepped forward until they formed a tight huddle.

Their bodies shielded their whispers from reaching the prison cell. Little did they know, their antics only brought a wave of relief through Talise's body. If they were nervous, it could only mean good things for her.

The short phrase she overheard gave her all the knowledge she needed anyway. First, the general had left. Second, if they worried for his safety, then maybe the base was under attack.

Or perhaps it was a rescue. After three weeks in the dungeon, she'd long since given up hope that someone would come to rescue her. But she *was* the princess. The possibility wasn't too much of a stretch.

She hadn't planned to escape like this. She was supposed to leave at night when most of the Kessoku were asleep. But if they were fighting, that might be even better. Nothing like the distraction of a fight for her to hide behind.

The guards fidgeted as they spoke.

She hadn't been up the stairs since her first escape attempt. She'd been going over the layout of the base in her mind ever since then, but there were still so many areas she knew nothing about.

An escape would still be risky, but this was as prepared as she'd ever get, and she knew it. Now it was time to do it.

Slipping a hand into her pocket, she pulled out the ice ball and hid it behind her back. She decided to start moaning about how dry her mouth was. If she gave the guards something to watch, they were less likely to notice her shaping ice behind her back.

With one hand, she levitated the ice ball above her palm. With a flood of fire through her veins, she made the ball melt into water. The water flowed gently into the shape of the key. She'd practiced it so many times, it whisked into shape with barely any thought.

That was good, since her ridiculous moaning noises took most of her brain power.

One of the male guards lifted his head from the huddle just so he could roll his eyes at her. Nothing in his body language suggested he realized she had anything behind her back.

When his head lowered back into the huddle, she smiled. She'd played her part well as the scared, pathetic princess. Her burlap tunic hung stiff with dried sweat. Her hair had been matted.

It still had the clumps of dirt she'd shoved into it the first day. Now it had even more dust that she'd added during her three weeks here.

Her face didn't have any cosmetics leftover from the masquerade ball, but she'd wiped enough dirt on it that it still looked frightening. Tear stains cut through the dirt on her cheeks. She couldn't see them, but she could feel the salty lines, and she was careful not to touch them.

Just as she hoped, she really did look pathetic.

Even her bare feet helped with the image, although she wished that part didn't have to be so authentic.

Time to break out. It would be slightly problematic because in all her planning, she counted on one guard being present. Not three.

Still, the opportunity was too good to pass up. Something was happening in the base, and that something would keep the Kessoku distracted.

With a silent breath, Talise began to freeze the key. The fire in her veins tempered the ice in her fingers, but this wasn't a normal freeze. The key had to be extra cold. Extra frozen. The colder the key, the more likely it would survive while turning the lock. She didn't have room for mistakes

With her ice shaping finished, her eyes swept across the dungeon corridor. How could she take out three guards instead of one? She usually had all four elements at her disposal. Since her last escape, the Kessoku had doused her cell and the surrounding corridor in flammable liquid. They hoped it would prevent her from using fire again. Since she wasn't an idiot, they hoped correctly.

They had also swept the dungeon corridor, so no extra dirt or stones lingered there. And even gathering enough water for the key had been a feat on its own. Which meant the only element available to her was air.

She'd have to get creative.

The dirt snake she made during the masquerade ball flashed through her mind. If she could make a snake from wind, maybe she could force the guards closer to her.

Shaping at that level of difficulty might be possible for her, but not immediately. It would take time and practice, neither of which she had now.

Another idea struck her that seemed too insane. She tried it anyway. At first, she was mostly curious about whether she could actually do it.

But then it started to work.

Pushing one hand in front of her, she reached out, feeling for the air that existed in the dungeon corridor. Then she reached upward, letting her sense of the air crawl up the stairs until she had reached the top of them.

Her sense ended at the top of the stairs. It probably wasn't possible to go much further than that in any circumstance, but maybe she'd practice again once she got out of prison.

Her next step took more effort. She grasped the air at the top of the stairs, then shaped it gently down the stairs. If the wind moved too quickly, the guards would know she used shaping to manipulate it. But if she did it slowly enough, hopefully they wouldn't realize what she had done.

Just as she hoped, the sounds from the top of the stairs suddenly seemed louder. Actually, they seemed closer, not louder exactly. It was like the sounds came from *on* the stairs instead of *up* the stairs.

Since the guards didn't realize she had shaped the noises closer, it probably sounded louder to them. Just like she wanted.

"What's going on?" one of them whispered in a voice loud enough to hear.

Soon, two of the guards disappeared up the stairs to investigate.

Perfect.

Just one left.

The female guard, Beady, stepped closer to the prison cell. Distrust filled her eyes to the rim. But fear spiraled through them too. "Is this because of you?" she asked.

"Is what because of me? What's happening up there?" Talise tried to look innocent, but maybe a gleam of excitement snuck onto her face because Beady immediately scowled.

"I'm not telling you anything. I won't fall for your tricks like the others do."

Talise shrugged. "I wasn't planning to make you fall at all. This time, I thought I'd try a gag."

Beady jumped back, which only poised her even closer to the strip of fabric Talise levitated behind her head.

Using air shaping that even Wendy would be proud of, Talise wound the cloth around Beady's mouth.

Another strip of cloth soon wound itself around Beady's wrists. Since Talise moved the cloth with air, she couldn't pull it as tight as she wanted, but it was good enough for now.

The shackles clanked around as she stuck her ice key into the lock on the iron bars. Now it was time to find out if she really had enough water.

The key turned, but when the lock began to click, Talise could sense cracks forming in the center of the ice key. As quickly as she could, she melted only the very center of the key, then refroze it. Hopefully that would repair the cracks.

A wave of cold burst through her fingers. For a brief moment, crystals seemed to form under the skin. Terror swept through her.

Frostbite? She'd been ice shaping for months and had avoided frostbite completely. She'd gotten so used to ice shaping, had she gone too far this time?

Had she made it too cold?

She didn't dare send fire any closer to her fingers for fear of melting the ice key. But she did heat the skin under her wrists to get her shackles glowing hot. That would have to be enough for now.

The torch clattered to the floor after some impressive thrashing by Beady. This sent an alarm through Talise, but she couldn't remember why. The lock held her mind's entire focus. Her breath hitched as she turned the key.

The lock clicked open.

Freedom.

Talise immediately sent fire through her fingers, but the crystals still seemed to sit just under the skin of her fingertips. They didn't feel like crystals anymore anyway. They felt like needles.

One last blast of ice swept through her hands before she clanged her shackles against the iron bars. Just like her last escape, they cracked half. She sent another wave of heat through her veins, eager to remove that frozen feeling from her fingertips. Nothing changed.

The heat around her didn't escape her notice, but she assumed it came from sending too much fire through her veins. But when she turned around, blazing flames burned through the corridor.

The torch. Beady had thrown the torch to the ground, and it had collided with the flammable liquid on the ground.

Everything around Talise burned. She had no water to douse the flames, and for the first time since she had learned it, she feared the consequences of shaping ice.

Just then, Beady's writhing form caught Talise's attention. The guard's wrists and mouth were still bound. The flames had nearly reached her.

Talise knew helping the guard would mean less time for her own escape. With a grunt, she rammed into the guard and forced her closer to the flames near the stairs. The guard's limbs flailed, but she wasn't strong enough to resist Talise's insistence. Or maybe the guard was simply too frightened to push back.

When the flames nearly licked the guard's face, Talise finally acted. She shaped her tiny ball of water into a spray of mist. This tempered the flames just enough so they wouldn't burn the guard. Beady made it safely through the flames to the staircase.

Talise stepped backward so the flames couldn't reach her. From the foot of the stairs, Beady eyed her carefully.

Talise had saved her life.

A flame roared between them. Now Beady was the one with a choice. Would she give Talise time to escape?

Even as the question entered her mind, Beady began to scramble up the stairs. Her eyes seemed intent on revenge rather than gratitude. No matter, Talise had a plan.

With any luck, the guards would put out the fire when they came down the stairs to catch her. That would help more than they knew.

Before she could think too much, she ran. Her feet slapped the stone corridor down the same path she took during her last escape attempt. With the flames roaring behind her, she easily ran faster than she had before. In almost no time at all, voices came from the staircase.

More guards would be down in the dungeon soon. She had to be out of sight by then. Her feet propelled her forward, but she kept her eyes pointing upward

All at once, she saw the small alcove in the ceiling. Her feet landed in an abrupt stop. She took in a deep breath. For some reason, her thoughts turned to Aaden. He would say this idea was insane. Ridiculous. The craziest thing she'd ever thought of. But he also would've believed she could do it.

She tried to hold onto that thought as she straightened her arms as stiff as rods. It had been impossible to practice this exact shaping technique in her cell since guards had been watching her constantly.

But she had been through the technique many times in her head. Hopefully it would be enough. With her arms still straight, she tilted her hands up until her palms were parallel to the ground.

Then, with as much force as she could muster, she shaped the air so that it shot out of her palms and hit the ground with great force. At first it did nothing and her heart dropped.

Closing her eyes, she dug deep inside. *Air shaping comes from the lungs* she said to herself. Filling her lungs with a heavy breath, the wind coming from her palms blew faster. And then, just as she had imagined in her head, her feet started to lift off the ground.

The further she got from the ground, the easier it was to keep rising. She shaped more air from around her and shot it to the ground. Had anyone ever shaped this way before? She wasn't flying exactly. It was more like hovering. But it felt like she could take on anything.

Soon, the ceiling was almost in reach.

Her spirits lifted the same as her body did. The clattering of swords and boots came down the hall, but it didn't matter. She was almost there.

Moments later, her fingertips reached for the alcove. Using a lip around the edge, she pulled herself inside just as boots pounded over the dungeon floor. Two dozen guards rushed through the corridor, just underneath her.

They shouted and growled, but not one of them bothered to look up.

And just like that, they had passed.

She was safe again.

Fearing the wind might be too loud, she decided to jump from the alcove and only use the wind shaping at the last second. Just enough to keep her ankles from cracking on point of impact.

Once on her feet, she could see the guards had put out the flames. Lucky her.

While the guards bounded down the corridor toward the chimney, she turned the opposite direction and headed up the stairs.

In her plans, Beady was supposed to be passed out on the ground so Talise could steal her clothes and blend in with the guards. Unfortunately, nothing had worked out the way she expected.

From here on out, she'd just have to wing it.

SIX

ESCAPING WITH BARE FEET HAD TO BE Talise's worst idea yet.

Each time her heel found a pebble, her muscles flinched in anger, and her brain kept screaming at her to slow down. Of course, she didn't.

This was her last chance to escape. If she didn't make it out now, surely Kessoku wouldn't bother keeping her prisoner anymore. They'd just kill her.

She bounded around a corner with her arms out, ready to shape if necessary. The upstairs corridors felt like a maze. Nearby Kessoku soldiers shouted and swore but not at her. In fact, they hadn't even noticed her. Whatever battle or attack was happening kept them fully engaged.

She didn't have time to find out what it was. All she could do was run.

When she tripped over a water bucket, a few of the soldiers started turning her way. She ducked behind the nearest corner, increasingly aware of her burlap tunic. The burlap must have been servant garb because none of the soldiers seemed to be wearing it.

Panting breaths escaped her as she ran down the latest corridor. She'd gotten turned around completely. All her plans to listen for noises outside that would help her find an exit were completely lost. It was too loud now. For a moment, she stopped in tracks.

The water bucket. It had been filled with water and she didn't do anything with it. She should have shaped some of the water to carry with her in case she needed a weapon. At the very least, she could have drunk some of it. She needed the strength.

With a small huff, she whirled around. Maybe her feet and her head were right about the need to slow down. She'd never escape if she moved without thinking about simple things like water. As she tiptoed down the corridor, a door flew open right in front of her.

She raised her hands to attack, but after the hovering earlier, weakness plagued her muscles.

A tall figure stepped through the doorway, his back to her. When she glimpsed the side of his goatee, she nearly slapped him across the face, just for existing. But when she looked closer, she realized. It wasn't Lucian in front of her.

Talise lunged forward, her arms around him in seconds. It didn't matter that she was holding onto him from behind. He was here and nothing could keep her back.

"Aaden," she breathed into his crisp silver uniform.

Only a second later, she realized he wasn't hugging her back. Maybe it was because she had grabbed onto him from such a strange angle, but maybe...

Immediately, she stumbled as she took several steps away. "Sorry," she said, brushing a matted strand of hair out of her face. She took another step back, unable to look up at him. "I must be filthy."

At the sound of her voice, she saw his feet turn toward her. He stepped forward until his boots brushed up against the sides of her feet. She dared to glance up. Disbelief shone bright in Aaden's eyes.

He cupped her cheek, tilting her head up. His eyes went from her cheeks to her ears, her forehead, and finally to her eyes. He kept brushing the hair out of her face even after all the strands were tucked well away.

Tears brimmed under his brown irises. He seemed to be holding his breath. When he swallowed, his jaw flexed. The scar across his eye had turned white. The pink of a fresh wound no longer colored it.

Finally, he let out a breath. He dropped his forehead until it met hers. "I was so scared." His voice was husky. He gulped again. "I thought for sure you'd be..."

His words failed him then. A single tear dropped from his lashes and onto her cheek.

Without another word, he wrapped her tight in his arms. He pulled her closer, resting her head against his chest where she could feel his heart thumping.

Before either of them could fully enjoy the embrace, the shouts of nearby Kessoku soldiers brought them back to the present moment. Aaden drew a sword from its sheath. He looked at Talise's empty hands with a frown.

"Can you shape?" he asked.

She bit her bottom lip. "My muscles are weak, and I'm dehydrated." And she was exhausted from her earlier hovering, but she'd tell him all about that when they had more time. Her head hung. "I don't know how much I can do."

Without a word, he pushed his sword into her hand while he reached into his boot. Soon, she held his sword, and he held a dagger with flames carved into the hilt. He nodded, but only took one step down the corridor before he looked down at the dagger. Then, he looked at his sword still in Talise's hands.

He looked back to his dagger again.

He seemed to be thinking the same thing as her.

She wanted to laugh, but with their enemy so near, it wasn't the best time. Without a word, they switched weapons. The weight of the dagger felt much better in her hand. Wendy had been right all along. Talise was a dagger person not a sword person.

A soft smirk lingered on Aaden's lips as they started down the corridor. It delighted her how they'd both been thinking the same thing.

Her thoughts turned again. If Aaden was here, and the base was under attack, then she'd been right. This was a rescue. But the sounds of battle raged, and now that Aaden was here, if they didn't escape, the Kessoku could have two prisoners to bargain with.

They couldn't get caught again.

SEVEN

TALISE AND AADEN RACED THROUGH the corridor. With thick boots on, Aaden didn't notice when his feet crunched over broken glass. Talise realized it a moment too late.

Her feet jumped in pain as the shards cut through her skin. She fell to the ground, unable to put any pressure on her feet. She plucked a glass shard from her heel, but many more remained.

Blood seeped out of her fresh wounds. Soon, it covered her feet, making it impossible to find the rest of the glass still embedded inside.

Aaden sucked in a breath. His jaw dropped at the sight of her bare feet. When the blood dripped onto the ground, he winced.

She bit her bottom lip as she reached for the hem of her tunic. "Maybe I can get something to…" Her voice trailed off as she tried to rip a strip from the burlap. The weakened muscles in her arms couldn't manage it. Suddenly, a woozy feeling spread through her. The ground tilted under her, and she couldn't tell if she was still sitting up.

How much blood had she lost? Or maybe her dehydration had kicked in.

A new figure appeared in the corridor with them. For a moment, it looked as if the man was going to bow to Aaden. His form stiffened when his eyes met Talise's. He pulled a sword from his side and charged forward.

Aaden struck him straight through the heart. Her blood loss must have been pretty serious because it seemed like the perfect moment to pull Aaden in for a kiss.

A shiver shook through her.

The past three weeks had been torture. She knew that. She had lived them. But she had hung on just enough to escape. But now her feet? She had one last thread holding her together, and it had snapped.

Everything unraveled. She had passed the limit of what she could handle.

Her body moved, but not because of anything she did. It took a moment to realize why. Aaden had lifted her into his arms. He was running.

The shouts around them grew louder, but then abruptly, they changed. Small chirps and rustling leaves joined the clash of swords.

Outside.

Aaden shouted. Suddenly, he set her down on top of something soft and bright white. They shouldn't have set her on something so clean. She'd spoil the linens in her dust-covered skin. Was that a strange thought to have a moment like this? Maybe.

The world went black.

But then it came back again, and everything was the same.

Except stars danced in her eyes.

Black.

Then white.

Was she inside a tent?

Why was the stone so soft? Wasn't she lying on stone? Or no, that wasn't right. She'd escaped. Right?

When she blinked, she let her eyelids rest for a moment. Just a little longer.

Liquid poured over her feet and her spine shot her straight up. Her teeth clenched together as needles seemed to slice through her legs.

"Lie back down." Aaden's voice was gentle, grounding. "You can squeeze my hand if it hurts too much."

He seemed to regret those words a moment later when another wave of liquid was poured over her feet. She squeezed so hard, his hand must've nearly broke. She clenched her teeth, suddenly remembering Kessoku. It probably wouldn't be good to scream out and give away their position. A small scream still escaped. She couldn't help it.

The liquid felt like acid. It seemed to eat away her skin and muscles until only bone remained. She checked four different times to make sure it hadn't. Through it all, Aaden's calm voice reassured her like a steady drum, grounding her and keeping her present.

It felt like hours had passed before the healers finished with her feet. While still working, one of the healers asked, "Do you have any other injuries?"

After feeling their remedies firsthand, she didn't really want to reveal her possible frostbite. The fear of losing her fingers won in the end. She raised her hand unsteadily.

"I think my fingertips are frozen."

The two healers pounced on her hand, staring at it with open mouths. One of them had a glint in her eyes. Talise wanted to rip her hand away and remind them she was not a science experiment. In the end, she didn't bother.

Aaden had started running his fingers along her forearm, and it thoroughly distracted her.

"You said you were dehydrated." She could hear the ache in his voice. "Did they starve you?" It wasn't like him to ask a serious question within the earshot of others. But, considering her recent kidnapping, they probably wouldn't get an abundance of privacy any time soon.

"No," she said, taking time to enjoy how the weight in his eyes lifted slightly. "Idiots," she added with a smirk.

He squeezed her hand in response. She decided not to tell him how they planned to start starving her that very day.

"They should have known it was only a matter of time before I escaped."

Aaden stroked her cheek as he smiled. It was a dangerous look. It made her forget other people existed.

A razor-sharp blade sliced over the tip of her finger, taking off a layer of skin with it. Talise yanked her hand back. The healer holding her wrist glared. Slowly, she extended her fingers once more, letting them do their work. She tried to sit still, but when the healer pulled off the skin from another finger, the pain bled through her. Her muscles seized as she fought to bear it.

"It's okay," Aaden whispered into her ear. He was stroking her hair now. "Just squeeze my hand when it hurts."

She had momentarily forgotten her free hand was still laced in his. It did feel better when she held it tight. Or maybe it just felt nice to have Aaden at her side.

The healers sliced another layer of skin off her pointer finger. She let out an involuntary gasp.

"Is this really necessary?" He offered a polite smile with the words, but Aaden spoke them through clenched teeth.

The nearest healer grunted, apparently too engrossed in his work to form words. The other said, "We have an ointment that will promote regrowth, but we have to remove all the dead skin first."

Despite her dehydration, small tears escaped through Talise's eyelids as another layer of skin was sliced away.

"Well," the tension in Aaden's voice pulled tight, "can't you hurry?"

Both healers glared in response. The news set Talise's muscles on edge. At least she only used one hand to make the ice key and not both of them.

Aaden leaned in closer. "It will be over soon. You're doing great."

She wanted to make some witty retort about how nothing about this was great, but the pain inhibited her ability to access wit. It was all she could do to keep from ripping her hand free of the healer's grip.

Luckily, Aaden was right. Before she knew it, the healers wrapped fluffy white gauze around each of her fingers. With everything finished, the pain already began to subside. Not normal, but better. And anyway, it would probably be a long while before she felt anything near normal.

Just as the healers left the tent, an anxious voice came from outside it.

"Why didn't anyone tell me earlier?" the hurried voice shouted.

Moments later, Wendy burst through the tent flaps with her hair in a messy braid. A slight sheen of sweat adorned her plump cheekbones. Her bright, black eyes looked Talise over from head to toe. At last, she let out a breath.

"Talise, you—" Suddenly, Wendy's nose wrinkled as she tried to cough away a gag, "smell awful."

Before Talise could chuckle, Aaden pulled her good hand against his chest. "It's not that bad."

Wendy clicked her tongue. "Yes, it is. You're just biased, so you don't notice."

Aaden's eyes narrowed as he pulled Talise's hand even closer.

Again, she fought back a chuckle.

"Don't worry," Wendy said, pulling a tent flap to the side. "I have buckets of warm water, lots of soap, and a few scrubbing tools. You'll be good as new in no time."

Aaden helped Wendy carry everything inside. Now fully conscious, Talise noticed she sat on top of a cot covered in a clean, white sheet. At the other side of the tent, two large tables stood with papers on top. She couldn't see past the tent flaps, but at least a few guards were probably standing nearby. Battle sounds tainted the air, which meant she hadn't been taken too far from the Kessoku's base.

Once Wendy set everything at the edge of Talise's cot, she waved Aaden toward the exit.

His lips pressed into a thin line. He folded his arms over his chest and planted both feet on the ground. "I'm not leaving."

Wendy let out an exasperated sigh. "In order to clean her, I have to undress her. I think the emperor would strangle you if he found out you were here for that part."

The determination in Aaden's eyes wavered for half a second. He reached for his elbow, squeezing it a little too tight. "What if something happens to her?"

Wendy brought two fingers to her forehead, impatience brimming in her eyes. "Do you know how many guards are standing outside this tent? Fifty. I counted them myself. You can join them if you like, but you need to be outside."

Aaden frowned, his feet unmoving.

Wendy's hands flew into the air with another exasperated sigh. "Do you *want* the emperor to strangle you?"

When he glanced back at Talise, his shoulder seemed to lean toward her involuntarily. He gulped, indecision still plaguing him. At last, he turned away. "Just promise you'll take care of her."

Wendy plastered a strained smile on her face before blinking twice. She waved him away again. When he didn't move, she flicked her hand against his arm until he started moving. She kept hitting him, speaking a word with each slap. "I have been her best friend ten times longer than you've even known her. I will take good care of her, I promise." She gave him one last shove.

The moment he finally disappeared behind the tent flap, Wendy let out an exaggerated groan. "He has been insufferable these past three weeks. You have no idea."

The chuckle that had been building in Talise's throat spilled out all at once. Soon, they were laughing. For the first time in too long, Talise's heart felt light.

It took three washings before Wendy declared the job finished. She said the smell still lingered, but after a few spritzes of perfume, she seemed satisfied.

Wendy even thought to bring clean linens, so Talise could lie down feeling as fresh and as clean as possible.

With the washing done, Wendy's face lost the look of purpose it had while working. It absorbed a new quality that seemed much darker than usual.

Did she wonder what the prison had been like?

Talise didn't want to discuss that topic yet. Since Aaden hadn't returned, she decided to use the moment to talk to the one person she trusted most.

Once her fingers landed on her friend's arm, Wendy froze in the middle of putting away a bottle of soap. She seemed to sense she should come closer. "What is it?" she whispered.

Talise pinched a piece of fabric between her fingers. The words rolled around in her mouth before she determined how to say them. "Have you ever heard of an amulet?" she asked, pinching the fabric tighter.

"Sure," Wendy said, returning to her task of putting the soap away. "Isn't it a pendant or some other kind of jewelry? Wait." Her eyes went wide.

"*Man* jewelry? Is it man jewelry that you're thinking about getting for..." She gave two meaningful glances toward the tent flaps as if pointing to them.

Talise waved her hands in front of her face while a blush crept into her cheeks. "No, it's nothing like that." She resisted the urge to fan the heat from her face. "I'm talking about a specific amulet. Something..." Her hand reached out as if trying to grasp the word she wanted from the air. When nothing came, she just said, "powerful."

Wendy shrugged as she carried the box of soaps over to the entrance of the tent. When she turned back to grab the water buckets, Talise swung her legs off the cot, so she could help.

After a heated glare from Wendy, Talise slowly moved her legs back.

Wendy moved the water buckets to the entrance before pouring something into a mug on one of the tables. With the mug in one hand, she twirled a small piece of hair through her other. "Didn't Kamdar have an amulet? He used it to give people shaping abilities or something."

Talise frowned. "I've never heard that."

Wendy pulled her lips into a tight knot as she twirled the hair even faster. "I thought I learned it in a history class, but maybe it was before I went to the elite academy in the Crown."

After several more seconds of staring off into space, Wendy shrugged. "We'll have to ask Claye when we get back to the palace. He loves doing research. And he always remembers the most obscure things. Here, drink this."

"Claye isn't here?" Talise asked as she took the mug of what turned out to be cool cider. The crisp liquid sent a flurry of cinnamon, nutmeg, and clove down her throat in a pleasant cascade. Her question suddenly seemed strange now that she thought about it. Why would Claye be there? With Aaden and Wendy nearby, maybe a part of her just felt like Claye should be there too.

Wendy showed the smallest hint of a scowl before it went back to its normal sweet look. "The emperor wouldn't let him come. He said because Claye is a *gardener* not a *soldier* and some other nonsense."

Talise let out a chuckle before leaning back into her cot. The pillow seemed even more comfortable than before. So did the cot. Or maybe they just felt nice because they weren't a stone floor. Whatever the reason, they seemed more comfortable than anything she'd ever known.

Her eyelids drifted closed for a second too long. She had to force them back open. "Can we go back to the palace now?"

Wendy shook her head. "No one knows your true identity." She let out a sweet shrug. "Except me, Claye, and Aaden, obviously. And whoever else already knew. In order to justify rescuing you, we've had to pretend the real goal was seizing control of the base. That's what the palace army is doing now."

"How can I help?" Talise's words ended in a long yawn. She'd just been racing through the corridors of Kessoku's base less than an hour before. She assumed her adrenaline wouldn't allow her to rest yet. But maybe all the exhaustion from the last three weeks had finally caught up with her.

Wendy brought a small stool over to the cot's side. Her eyes were suddenly anxious. "You didn't see Cyrus, did you?"

It felt like wading through mud as Talise brought her mind back to the conversation. These words needed her full attention, but each second it was more difficult to keep her eyes open. "I didn't see him. I didn't see anyone from the palace."

Hopefully she conveyed at least a smidgeon of the sympathy in her heart.

Wendy's expression turned indifferent. "It's fine. We know this isn't Kessoku's main base. We're still in the Crown. We know they have at least one base in the Gate. According to latest intelligence, they might have a few. The other prisoners are probably there."

Talise tried to swallow over the lump in her throat. She wanted to believe that as much as Wendy did, but she'd also seen how they treated their prisoners. The only reason Talise had been kept alive was for information. The other prisoners had been killed within hours.

The cot seemed eager to swallow her. With a heave, she tried to sit up. "Where's that dagger? Aaden gave me a dagger on our way here. I just need to get some shoes on, and I can go join the battle."

Wendy laughed as she pushed Talise back into the bed. "You're not going anywhere, especially not with your feet cut up. You are staying here until you've slept through the night. The fifty guards outside will make sure you stay put in case you get any ideas."

Her eyes were fluttering closed again, but she managed to clench her jaw and let out an angry huff.

Apparently, her effort made Wendy giggle. With a sweet smile that looked slightly devious, she said, "Besides, that sleeping draught I gave you should be kicking in right about now."

Talise didn't bother sitting up since it felt like her shoulders were filled with wet sand. She did manage to shoot an accusatory frown at her friend. "The *what* you gave me?"

"Emperor's orders," Wendy replied with a wink.

While Talise tried to arrange her sleeping face into a scowl, Aaden appeared and shooed Wendy away. He ran his fingers through Talise's hair, which felt much nicer than she expected.

She wanted to accuse him too. She wanted to use her most fiery voice and ask if he also knew about the sleeping draught. But sleep tickled at the edge of her mind making her mouth betray her. In a mumbled voice she asked, "Now that I'm all clean, don't you want to kiss me?"

Aaden let out a light chuckle. That smile could have kept her alive through any amount of starvation.

"Yes," he said, letting his fingers slide through her hair. "But not while you're falling asleep like this. Tomorrow. After you've rested."

His last words felt like a dream, beckoning her into a deep and peaceful sleep.

EIGHT

THE WALL WAS COMING DOWN. Behind it, a storm raged.

Talise knew she was dreaming because the wall had a shimmery quality along with a slight blue glow. Crowds of people surrounded her, but none of them had distinct faces.

Her clothes were even more dream-like. She wore a dark purple gown with silver crescent moons threaded through the silk in a rich brocade pattern. The skirt was ridiculous. Its train trailed at least three dress lengths behind her.

The wide bell sleeves fell down past her feet. Every few seconds, she pushed the sleeves up to her elbows, but they'd fall back down almost immediately.

Most conspicuous, her head felt heavy under the weight of a crown. The thick belt around her waist had been pulled tight, making it difficult to breathe.

She was a princess.

Just as the thought came to her, a strong grip tugged her by the wrist. The folds of her gown tripped her with each step, but the tugging at her wrist only grew more insistent. Talise glanced through the crowd, trying to see where she was being pulled.

Between heads, she could barely make out a small squadron of soldiers, each wearing a tunic with a yellow hem. Her soldiers.

She gasped and glanced back at the wall. Her heart stopped at the sight of it. Danger. The word gripped her, shook her as she stared. Pieces of the wall crumbled to the ground. Some spots looked ready to burst apart.

Bad. This was bad.

Talise ached to rush toward her soldiers. They would need her protection once the wall came down. All at once, the figure pulling her along became distinct. Not just a random person from the crowd. It was... her.

Her?

She pulled herself, but this version of her wore a silk tunic and training pants. This part was the Master Shaper.

Before she could even imagine what that meant, another figure grabbed her other wrist and tugged her the opposite way. The second figure was just a child, but she dug her nails into Talise's wrist, forcing her to take a few steps in the desired direction.

The glittering tiara and orange velvet dress gave her identity away much sooner than the other. This was Princess Talise.

Master Shaper Talise tugged on the left while Princess Talise dug in her nails on the right. Each pulled her in opposite directions, turning the dream world into a hazy fog. She blinked away the tears that burned her eyes and tried to ignore the tugging.

The wall.

Didn't they understand? The wall was coming down. It didn't matter if she was a Master Shaper or a princess. She had to stop the wall from coming down.

She only managed one painful step forward before the wall crumbled before her. Exultant shouts cried out as the wall fell like dust to the earth. The storm behind it thundered and shook the ground.

Her eyes narrowed as she tried to make out who was so happy. The figures around the wall blurred, but one figure she recognized.

Lucian Sato punched a fist into the air while a wide smile split across his face. The others around him wore Kessoku's symbol on their backs.

They knocked the wall down. They had freed the storm.

The tugging at Talise's wrists grew more insistent. Master Shaper Talise wanted her to fight with the soldiers. Princess Talise wanted her to give a speech at the emperor's side.

They both seemed to think their needs were most important, but only Talise understood what was about to happen. She took a step back. Then another.

More.

She tripped over the swaths of fabric behind her, but it didn't stop her from backing away.

Even as she moved, she knew it wouldn't save her from the onslaught.

As the Kessoku cheered, figures appeared among the mist of the storm. They hardly looked like people at all.

Their teeth jutted out in long, sharp fangs. Animalistic claws grew straight from their knuckles. They didn't speak. Instead, they let out hisses and spits. They attacked everything around them without any hesitation.

Claws ripped through the Kessoku until their symbols had been painted with blood. Fangs ripped through muscles and bone.

Her soldiers were falling. Citizens were falling. Kessoku was falling.

The animal people let out growls and turned their attacks onto each other. Their eyes glowed gray and blue with flashes of white. Exactly like a storm.

Terror gripped Talise as she watched people fall on every side. The storm people frightened her the most, but then, nobody liked people from the Storm.

They were dangerous. Criminals.

She tried to run. Her feet had melded to the ground. Her heart raced.

They were coming.

She held her breath, waiting for the thrashes, the slices. The death.

Then, a new person appeared. This one didn't have a figure. She was nothing more than a voice in Talise's ear. A memory.

"You must help them, love."

A voice of honey and sparkles.

Marmie.

Who? Talise wanted to shout. Her mouth hung open, urging the word forward, but it wouldn't come. Tears streamed down her face while every muscle inside her froze.

Who do I help?

As Master Shaper, her duty belonged to her soldiers. As princess, she owed her allegiance to the emperor, to the crown.

But long ago, she'd been a citizen of the Storm. Did she owe something to them? Those people *were* dangerous, but only because they were desperate. It wasn't their fault. Was she supposed to help them?

How could she choose?

And what about Kessoku? Surely Marmie didn't think *they* deserved help. She couldn't possibly want Talise to aid her enemy.

An animal-man with stormy eyes growled as he approached her. Black coated his mouth while black veins spread out around it.

I'll help you. She tried to say it, but her throat had filled with sand.

The man howled as he took his claws to her dress. Pain dropped onto her stomach, causing her to wake with a start.

NINE

"SORRY!" A GIRL GRABBED A HEAVY scroll from off of Talise's stomach as more apologies spewed from her lips. "I was trying to put it away in this chest, and it slipped out of my grasp."

Sleep weighted Talise's eyelids down. Her heart still raced from the horrific dream. The edges of the room slowly came into focus as she blinked.

After rubbing her eyes, everything became easier to see.

A tent. She was inside of a tent. Sleeping on a cot.

She let out a breath of relief as memories of the day before came back to her. She'd been rescued.

Even though it had ended, the dream kept her heart pounding. She forced herself to focus on the present moment.

The girl who dropped the scroll didn't have Wendy's sweet smile or bright eyes.

Instead, she wore a soldier's tunic with a blue hem. One of the better soldiers, except still one of Talise's. In fact, it was the same soldier who had defied her in front of the emperor, but who later trusted Talise enough to tell her about the Kessoku spies in the ballroom.

"Tempest," Talise said as she sat up.

Tempest's eyebrow raised. "You remember my name?"

Laughing seemed like an appropriate response. How could she forget? Emotional memories were the easiest to remember and every interaction with Tempest always seemed to have so much emotion. But even as Talise tried to laugh, it wouldn't come.

The haunting shadow of Marmie's voice still lingered at the back of her mind. Competing allegiances fought inside her, no matter how she tried to ignore them.

"Where is Aaden?" Talise expected a protest when she swung her legs off the cot, but Tempest seemed to welcome it. "And Wendy. She's my friend. Do you know Wendy?"

A hint of a smile appeared on Tempest's face. "She's inside the base. So is Aaden. So is practically everyone." With a bit of a scowl she added, "Except me."

"Can we join them?" Talise leaned forward as she asked, gripping the side of the cot a little too tight.

For a moment, Tempest's eyes lit up. A moment later, her face fell, and she let out a groan. "No, we have orders to stay here. They said you need to recover."

Judging by the face Tempest made, she didn't seem overjoyed about being chosen to stay back.

Talise grinned. She could use that.

"Do you know where they are? What they're planning?"

Tempest hopped off the stool and showed her first real smile. Pointing to a diagram on one of the tables, she said, "It's all right here. They sent in a scout yesterday after Aaden found you. The scout created a map of the base, and he found this awesome tunnel thing that leads from the dungeon corridor down to their main strategy room. That's where all the top Kessoku members are now. We have soldiers fighting outside the base, but the real fight is going to start in about an hour. A squadron is going down the tunnel to surprise the Kessoku."

Tempest looked enormously pleased with herself as she finished the explanation.

With each of the words, Talise's heart jumped higher into her throat. She ran a finger over the tunnel and down one of the mapped corridors.

"Is this the dungeon?" Talise asked, pointing to the paper.

Tempest took the diagram into her hands and turned it sideways. She mouthed a few words while nodding at different rooms on the map. With a curt nod, she said, "Yes, it is."

Take a breath. Talise put one hand over her forehead as she forced herself to suck in air and let it out slowly.

When finished, she scanned the room. First, she needed clothes. She couldn't wear the soldier uniform Wendy had given her yesterday.

At the end of her cot, her burlap prison clothes were tossed on top of some boots.

Perfect.

She stripped down to her underclothing and went straight for the burlap.

Behind her Tempest stood eerily still. "Um, what are you doing?"

Before Tempest finished the sentence, Talise already had the prison clothes on. She reached for the boots and pulled them on in time to get a whiff of the clothes. *Blech.*

They really did smell awful.

Pain nudged through the cuts on her feet as she pulled on the boots but not too much for her to handle.

Tempest's foot began tapping on the dirt ground of the tent. "Remember when I said we have orders to stay here? I'm not supposed to let you leave."

Talise spared her a single glance. "That tunnel leads to an incinerator. Once they go down, the only way out is to go back up. By the time they realize what the tunnel is, Kessoku soldiers will be at the top waiting for them, and a bonfire will be at the bottom ready to burn them alive."

When she stood, Tempest was squeezing her forearm. She stared at the ground. "Do you think they could get hurt then?"

Talise shook the linens on her cot, hoping to find the dagger Aaden had given her the day before. "Definitely."

After shaking the linens again, Talise noticed the dagger sitting just under her cot, as if it had been placed there with care. The fluffy gauze on her fingers stretched as she plucked it up.

"But," Tempest said while squeezing her forearm again, "I have orders to keep you here."

The dagger fit perfectly in the little belt Talise fashioned from a strip of extra linen. "Do you want them to die?"

"No."

"Then you'll let me go." She marched toward the tent entrance expecting no resistance.

Tempest caught her by the wrist, which sent her back to her dream for a single frightening moment. Shaking away the memory, Talise glanced back at her soldier.

Tempest had a bit of her lip stuck between her teeth. "I don't want them to die, but I have to follow orders."

Talise pulled her wrist free and let out a sigh. Her heart started to sink, but in a flash, the world brightened. "Who gave you the orders? The emperor? General Gale?"

The soldier shook her head slowly, as an idea seemed to be sprouting in her mind. "No, it was Master Shaper Aaden who gave the order."

A smile grew on Talise's face at the same rate as her soldier's. "Well, I'm a Master Shaper, too, am I not?"

Tempest's smile continued to grow as she nodded.

With a smirk, Talise said, "As Master Shaper, I'm giving you new orders. You are to stay here while I rescue the others."

"Oh." Tempest's shoulders fell as she dropped her eyes to the ground. "I thought you would want my help." She turned around and wrapped a hand over one of her elbows.

Talise blinked. "It would require water shaping. I know the fire balls were difficult for you. I don't want to ask something of you that would be too difficult."

With a twirl, the soldier turned around, her eyes beaming. "I know my fire shaping is dismal, but water is my primary." Her chest puffed up. "I can collect rainfall for three hours before I get tired."

Excitement caught on fire inside Talise's toes. "Perfect. We just need to find you some new clothes."

TEN

IN THE END, TALISE GAVE THE PRISON clothes to Tempest. Neither of them loved the idea, especially because it meant Tempest had to endure the smell of Talise's three weeks in prison. But neither one of them could think of another way for Talise to sneak past the fifty guards outside the tent.

Talise's chin-length hair would be a problem. She braided it as well as she could, but it didn't look close to her soldier's typical long braid. Hopefully the guards would be too bored to notice. She snatched the diagram of the Kessoku's base from off the table and buried her head in it.

Her boots fell heavier than usual as she marched out of the tent. The pain from her cuts skittered across her feet with each step. If she showed the slightest sign of hesitation, the guards might recognize her. They might recognize her anyway but acting like Tempest had to count for something.

She held her breath the whole way. A few steps outside the tent, one of the guards did call after her. "Where are you going? You're supposed to stay with Master Shaper Talise."

Her throat constricted. Would they recognize her voice if she responded? Tempest had been easy to convince, but could she convince fifty other guards to defy orders and let her into the base?

"Eat flames, Phoenix. I'm just getting her a drink."

The voice came from the tent, but it was Tempest's voice. *Phoenix* apparently didn't seem to notice the odd direction. From behind her, Talise heard a soft chuckle. She squared her jaw and kept marching forward.

Once she passed the large tent, she snuck into an area of the Kessoku base that had already been seized by the palace army. Talise pulled the diagram drawn by the palace scout from her pocket. Her finger traced over a small room labeled *Servant Quarters*.

She frowned at the door in front of her.

It was a risk going into the quarters before the base had been officially seized. But Tempest insisted the army already had control of this part of the base, so there shouldn't be any servants inside.

With a deep breath, Talise pushed open the door. She let out a breath at the sight of the empty room before her. It didn't take long to find an extra pair of servant clothes to change into.

A few minutes later, Tempest burst in through the doorway with a maniacal grin on her face. "They're looking for you. But I told them you wanted to go back to the palace, so they're looking in the wrong direction."

Talise raised an eyebrow. "Remind me not to get on your bad side."

"You already did," Tempest said with a laugh. "As I recall, it didn't work out too well for you."

Wincing in pain, Talise stuffed her foot into a boot while wearing her new servant garb. She glanced up at Tempest, barely suppressing the grin on her face. For someone who so adamantly followed orders, Tempest definitely had a devious side.

"Come on," Talise said. "We need to find water buckets and get down to the strategy room."

TALISE HAD SMEARED gobs of dirt over her face, but it still felt like the Kessoku soldiers all stared at her. With each step down the tight corridor, their eyes seemed to pierce her skin. At any moment, she could pass one of the guards who had watched over her in the prison cell. They could recognize her. At any moment, she could be caught.

The balls of her feet hit the stone with each step but not her heels. Each time they got close, her heels would bounce, forcing her heart in her throat again.

"Did you hear about the princess?" one of the soldiers whispered.

Talise nearly froze. How could it be a coincidence that a guard talked about her right as she came near?

The Kessoku guard's voice didn't waver as she kept walking. He punched a fellow guard while wearing a wide grin. "The general asked if she had ever seen Emperor Kamdar's gravestone, and she said yes."

The guard next to him rolled his eyes. "She's gone, remember? What good is it if we can't even use her to find the gravestone?"

"It means the amulet is real." Hope glimmered in the guard's eyes.

Hope.

That was a word she hadn't thought about in a long time. It reminded her of a letter from Marmie, but she couldn't remember exactly why.

"Stop dreaming." The second guard jabbed his friend in the shoulder. "Just because the gravestone is real doesn't mean the amulet is."

The first guard's eyes took on another layer of hope. "It has to be. The amulet is our only chance to win this war."

The second guard looked ready to jab his friend again, but he seemed to notice how Talise's steps had slowed.

"Hey!" he shouted in a gruff voice.

Her head dropped as she shuffled forward. The guard yanked her by the wrist until she stood right in front of him. Still, she kept her head down. Her heart thumped wildly.

Tempest's boots knocked into Talise's, but the guard waved her on. "Not you. You go ahead."

The ground crunched as Tempest backed away. The guard's grasp began to burn around Talise's wrist. He scowled. "I swear, the people in Kamdaria keep getting stupider."

The lump in Talise's throat hardened. The room had too many people for her to run from. With Tempest's help, she could take on at least half the guards. Maybe after that, they'd get a chance to run.

"Look at that blank expression." The guard snarled at her as he spoke. "Do you have anything inside that brain, little servant?"

Talise blinked. She assumed he had recognized her, but now? "D... did you want something?"

Her voice wavered with each word, which seemed to prove whatever point the guard was making. He lifted her wrist higher until it hung level with his eyes. Only at that moment did she realize he had grabbed the hand that held the water bucket.

"Oh!" Talise quickly nodded and dropped the wooden ladle inside the bucket. Did the other servants usually shape the water out of the ladle?

Before she could ask, the guard snatched the ladle out of her hand and dumped the water onto his head. He let out a quiet sigh, then did it again.

Her jaw clenched. Her fingers wanted to form fists, but that would probably look a little suspicious. Instead, she curled her toes inside of her boots until they ached in pain.

She needed that water.

It took everything in her not to shape it out of the guard's hair and put it back in the bucket where she needed it.

At last, he dropped the ladle into the bucket with a sneer. "Don't forget to offer water to the other guards. He caught her wrist again. "And no more eavesdropping, or I'll tell the general to send you back to the Storm."

She couldn't get away from him fast enough. Soon, she scuttled just behind Tempest as they continued down the crowded corridor. His words stuck inside her like sap.

The Storm? That's where they got their servants? So Lucian hadn't lied about that, after all. No wonder they got away with treating their servants so badly. If the alternative was the Storm, they'd probably be willing to endure anything.

She pushed the thoughts to the back of her mind. That was yet another thing she'd have to consider once she got back to the palace. That list had almost grown too long to endure at this point.

Aaden's father worked for Kessoku. Kessoku was looking for an amulet that could supposedly give them the power to win a war. Kessoku had someone working in the palace that may or may not have been one of her friends.

Her head visibly shook side to side, and one of the guards gave her an odd look. No. It wasn't one of her friends. She had gone over the evidence enough times. The betrayer could have been anyone.

Once she caught up to Tempest, it didn't take long to reach the end the of the corridor. They slipped into the shadows without much trouble. Perhaps being a servant did have some benefits. Nobody treated her with dignity dressed as she was in these clothes, but they hardly noticed her either.

The entrance to the strategy room didn't have a door. Instead, a large archway had been cut through the stone. The room it led to had large couches and tables with simple furnishings.

There were no guards standing in the archway.

Maybe it was a message. Maybe Kessoku wanted its people to believe there were no secrets. Anyone would be welcome in the strategy room at any time.

That seemed like such a foreign concept to Talise, who had grown up smothered by lies. Thinking of a world without them felt both intriguing and terrifying.

As they inched forward, more of the room came into focus. A dozen Kessoku soldiers bent over a large table as they whispered with each other. Talise looked for Lucian first, still desperate for any kind of revenge.

He wasn't there. As one of the Kessoku guards had said earlier, he must have left long ago.

She turned to Tempest, pulling the bucket of water closer to her chest. "Are you ready?"

ELEVEN

THE ARCHWAY INTO THE STRATEGY
room provided the perfect cover. Talise and
Tempest crouched to one side so they could shape
the water out of their buckets and onto the floor.

According to the plans Tempest had
overheard, they still had a few minutes before the
palace squadron arrived down the chimney.

"Is that it?" Tempest whispered as she pointed
to the back corner of the room. A short wall only
a few bricks high had been built to enclose the
corner. Inside the short wall, stacks of wood
reached almost as high as the ceiling.

A small pile of clothes and papers sat next to
the wall, probably waiting to be incinerated.
Maybe the clothes had worn out that was the
purpose for burning them. Or maybe they were

evidence of some kind. If the chance came up, she'd try to save the items to go through them.

At the moment, more pressing information stole her attention.

The bonfire wasn't lit.

Fear clenched inside of Talise at this observation. She hoped the incinerator would be burning, then the palace squadron would realize the danger before climbing all the way down. But now?

They would get to the end of the chimney, the Kessoku would light the fire, and they would burn before they had a chance to climb back up. For the few who managed to escape the flames, the Kessoku would send soldiers to meet them at the top. They'd be killed the moment they exited the chimney.

That realization only deepened Talise's resolve. Maybe she had defied orders, but that entire squadron—including Wendy and Aaden— would soon be dead if she hadn't. Princess Talise wouldn't approve. But Master Shaper Talise did.

Turning back to her soldier, Talise shaped a small ball of water from the water bucket. "They'll probably use fire shaping to light the wood as soon as they hear people coming down the chimney. Hopefully our people get down pretty far before that happens."

Tempest nodded. "And then we'll shape a water dome over the fire to protect them, and you'll turn some of it to ice, so they can slide down the side."

Talise nodded without a smile. She doubted things would work out as easily as they planned. For one thing, ice shaping concerned her. The tips of her fingers still throbbed from the healers' treatment on her frostbite. But it was too late to second guess anything. Now, she could only focus on protecting the palace squadron.

She shaped the small ball of water from the bucket and straight onto the stone floor. Before it could seep into the stone, she moved it so it would slide across the stone almost like a stream.

Except it wasn't really like a stream at all because she kept the water just above the stone so it wouldn't flow. She and Tempest needed to get their water from the buckets over to the incinerator, and they had to do it without any of the dozen Kessoku noticing.

Tempest leaned onto the balls of her feet as she watched the water glide over the stone floor.

Talise moved it slowly enough to look like a water spill, except the puddle moved.

Still on the balls of her feet, the soldier slowly raised the water out of her own bucket. It lowered to the ground in a sweeping movement, devoid of any jerkiness.

Impressive.

For the first time ever, Talise wondered if her soldier had gotten a place in the palace the same way Wendy had. Because of her shaping.

Soon, the two puddles slithered silently over the stone. Not one member of the Kessoku had noticed it yet.

When they finally got the water close enough, Talise's stomach clenched in terror. The piles of wood dwarfed their two tiny puddles. Maybe it would be better to abandon their plan and douse the wood now. Except, they didn't have enough water for that much wood.

Besides, with strong enough fire shaping, the Kessoku could dry out the wood in no time. Before she could consider any other ideas, noises trickled down from the chimney.

The Kessoku noticed at the same time she did. It only took one hurried whisper before three of them lit the wood into burning flames.

Tempest grinned wildly. "Let's do this."

Talise formed the dome with ease, especially with Tempest's help. But the fire began turning the water to steam within seconds. Still, the water must have shielded the people inside the chimney from at least some of the heat.

Shouting echoed through the room.

It wasn't clear if the shouting came from the chimney, the Kessoku or both, but there was little time to figure it out. And there was little point in hiding. The Kessoku knew the water came from somewhere. They'd find her and Tempest soon enough.

Rather than wait for the inevitable, Talise marched out from behind the archway. She kept the water dome in place with her right hand and held the flame-carved dagger in her left. When two Kessoku came near, she sneered as she raised the dagger toward them.

"By order of the emperor, you will all surrender." She raised the dagger again as if to make her point.

Her tenacity definitely surprised them. That was something at least. But it didn't take long to begin an attack.

Five of them drew swords and another four raised their hands, ready to shape. The others scuttled to the other side of the room where Tempest stood.

Talise decided to ignore them. She couldn't fight off all twelve of them anyway. Hopefully Tempest could handle the rest.

Before she could get her bearings further, one of the Kessoku punched fire balls toward her. Another sent a wall of wind. She dodged them both, but the fire caught the hem of her tunic. A flame burned at her waist.

She dropped to the ground in a tight roll, letting the stone floor smother the flame as she moved. Keeping her right hand out, she just managed to keep the water dome in place. When she got back to her feet, she shaped a wall of wind at the Kessoku while she ran toward the chimney.

They dodged her wall as easily as she had avoided theirs. But she had no time to think about that now. More shouts rang through the room, and those ones definitely came from the chimney.

The water dome shimmered as it began to lose integrity. Fire flooded her veins as she prepared to shape ice. The moment the cold split through her, needles of pain stabbed into her fingers where the frostbite hadn't finished healing.

Without a second thought, she tossed the dagger into her right hand and tried shaping ice with her good hand instead. But her fingers shook, and her heart beat too wildly. She couldn't tell how much heat to use. She couldn't feel how much cold she needed.

With a gulp, she accepted the truth. No more ice shaping, At least for now.

She nodded to herself and began running through new ideas in her head. Considering the situation, she thought she handled the news with a fair amount of cool.

Someone jumped onto her back and held a knife to her neck, which ripped her focus from the dome for a split second.

Her knees collapsed. While the knife blade flirted with her throat, her eyes fixated on the water dome. Or where it should have been.

Nothing remained but the flames now licking high into the chimney.

She lost concentration for only a moment when the Kessoku jumped onto her back. But it had been enough. Too much. The dome of water fell into the fire, which left the palace squadron unprotected.

Her heart jumped into her throat.

That reminded her of the knife still lodged against it. *Deal with the knife first*. She couldn't do anything to help her soldiers with a blade at her throat.

Her elbow sank into the Kessoku man's gut. He grunted but didn't release the grip of his knife. Crushing the top of his foot with her boot seemed like the next logical step, though it did send a fresh slice of pain through the cuts on her feet.

It also forced a gasp from her attacker. He didn't let go, but his grip loosened just enough for her to twist around.

The heel of her hand jammed into his nose in an upward motion. Finally, the knife dropped to the ground as the man took chaotic steps backward. By the time he reached up for his nose, drips of blood already drained out of it.

More Kessoku ran toward her, but she sent another wave of wind at them. With so much desperation grinding through her insides, it wasn't difficult to create a stronger wind than before. This one knocked them all off their feet.

Tempest fought on the other side of the room. Her movements involved a sword, but Talise didn't have a spare second to look closer.

Her eyes turned back to the fire. Small flames near the top wisped upward in a strange motion before they would vanish. Suddenly, a memory of the masquerade ball came back to her. Wendy had saved her from two fire arrows by shaping the air away from them so they couldn't burn.

Now Wendy must have been doing it again.

Talise grinned. With even more force than she used on the wall of wind, she sucked the air away from the fire.

The oxygen starvation didn't work as well as she wished, but it did temper the flames greatly. For a moment, they lowered to tiny flames.

With her feet planted on the ground, she raised her hands to do it again. The second time, the flames turned to embers.

Two people jumped from the chimney onto the glowing wood, which sent sparks flying everywhere. She thought she recognized Aaden's goatee, but a moment later someone had grabbed her by the waist.

Without thinking, she swung her dagger back until it sank into flesh. She felt her mouth twist in horror as she rounded on her heel to see who she had stabbed. The Kessoku man gripped his shoulder while gnashing his teeth.

She ripped the dagger from his body, but a second later, her body slammed forward onto the stone. Twisting her body, she rolled onto her back with her face forward. A Kessoku guard with two broken teeth towered over her. He aimed his slim sword straight for her heart. His boots shoved her arms so they were pinned at her sides.

Wriggling seemed like her only available tactic, but that wouldn't get her far.

Her breath caught in her throat. This was it.

TWELVE

THE THIN SWORD ABOVE TALISE glinted in the light. Her shoulders moved side to side, trying to free herself from the Kessoku soldier's grasp. It wasn't enough.

As his sword dove toward her, a large stone crashed into it, forcing it off its course until the tip clanged against the stone floor. Before the soldier could react, Aaden tackled him to the ground. A palace guard Talise didn't recognize stuck a sword through the Kessoku's uniform, piercing his heart.

The palace guard turned without a second glance, already focused on his next target. Aaden jumped to his feet and offered a hand to Talise.

Her heart was still galloping like horses, but at least it didn't have a sword through it.

"You're supposed to be resting," Aaden said as he pulled her to her feet.

She glanced back at the glowing embers as she brushed the dirt off her tunic. "If I had stayed back in the tent, you'd be dead now. I think what you meant to say was *thank you*."

His grin made her heart jump, but at least it jumped in delight instead of terror. She moved closer to the chimney to get a better look inside it. "Is everyone down yet?"

Even as she asked, two more palace soldiers jumped down from the small opening. A small burst of wind kept the fire sparks from spreading too far.

"That was the last of this group. We have another group coming, but they're trying to seize one of the rooms upstairs first." Aaden had drawn his sword. His grip looked tighter than usual. Apparently, even he could forget proper grip in a dire enough situation.

For a moment, the world seemed calm. As calm as it could be under the circumstances, at least. With the arrival of the palace soldiers, most of the Kessoku were already dead. The others fought hard, but it wouldn't be long before the palace soldiers had control.

Her eyes danced around the room in a gut-wrenching panic as she saw a woman with shiny cheeks fall under a sword. After jerking toward the fight, she realized with relief that the woman wasn't Wendy. Her best friend stood in the corner fighting off a Kessoku with a clump of dirt and a small tornado.

Wendy clearly had the upper hand.

Aaden rested his hand on her back. It felt nice to lean into his touch instead of cowering from it as she had spent pointless months doing. With a growing grin, he asked, "How did you get past—"

"Duck!"

Tempest's voice cut through the stillness just as an arrow whooshed past Talise's ear. Aaden yanked her toward the ground as he drew his sword. Three more arrows shot through the air while Talise fumbled to grip her dagger.

Palace guards trampled toward the new threat, but more Kessoku archers spilled into the room from the stone archway. After a single blink, two of the palace soldiers were dead.

Even more Kessoku soldiers poured into the room, each carrying weapons poised and ready to kill. Another palace soldier fell before Talise could finally get a grip on her dagger.

On her hands and knees, she crept toward the Kessoku soldiers, ducking behind tables as she moved. Another wave of men wearing Kessoku's symbol burst into the room.

One archer pointed an arrow at Wendy and Talise moved without thinking. Her left hand shaped a circle of wind. It shook so much it was difficult to keep the wind crown steady.

When the archer pulled back the string on his bow, Talise's arm acted on its own. She threw the dagger into her wind crown. The Kessoku man collapsed to the ground the moment her dagger sank into his heart.

His bow clattered to his side with the arrow still in place. Her heart stopped.

She had used the dust trick to ensure Kessoku soldiers died back at the palace. She had been standing right next to Kessoku soldiers and palace soldiers as they met their death.

But this. This was her first kill.

It ripped her heart in two. It shred her soul to pieces. A single action but one that had changed her forever.

Aaden pulled her back behind a table. For a moment, she had forgotten about him. He took her hand and held it against his chest. "You did it for Wendy," he said.

And then her heart started again. It took one slow beat. And then another. The pulses felt too weak, but then it all changed, and they felt too strong. Too heavy.

Her head fell as she nodded.

The warmth in Aaden's hand brought her back to reality again. He squeezed gently and brought her fingers to his lips.

"For Wendy," she repeated, though the words felt like dust in her mouth. She cleared her throat. "And for Kamdaria."

Aaden's smile had vanished, his eyes were already back on the fight. No matter how her heart squeezed, they had already wasted too much time behind that table. Her jaw clenched as she jumped back into the fight.

Talise shaped walls of wind whenever she could. She blasted fire balls into as many interlocking circle uniforms as she could find. She didn't want to kill. But just like at the palace, Kessoku made the fight necessary.

She whirled around on her feet, sending fire balls all around her. She felt Aaden at her back, his sword swinging in one hand while the other he used for shaping.

A Kessoku soldier used two swords to fight. Talise slammed a wall of wind against her. When the soldier's back hit the ground, it knocked the wind out of her.

With the soldier out of the way, Talise noticed a pair of Kessoku she hadn't seen before. Two willowy Kessoku, one man and one woman, scuttled through the room on their tiptoes, just missing the blades and fireballs that sliced through the air.

But they didn't just prance around with no intent. Each of them gathered papers and maps from off the tables.

Talise shaped a large stone from a corner of the room and slammed it into the nearest Kessoku's gut. This gave her room to get a closer look at what the two Kessoku gathered. They took most of the papers from the tables, but they checked underneath before pocketing them.

Were they looking for something?

Talise blew an oncoming Kessoku soldier off his feet as she stalked even closer.

"I got the prison records," the man whispered as he tucked a leather-bound notebook into his tunic. The leather had been embossed on the front with a design that looked like a gate. But from so far away, Talise couldn't tell for sure.

"We still need the amulet research." Panic laced the woman's voice as she lifted another set of papers off a nearby table. Her eyes lit up. "*Here* it is."

Another leather-bound notebook sat in her hands. This leather looked much softer, as if old and worn from frequent use. The front didn't have a fancy embossing like the other. But it did have a symbol scratched onto its surface.

A circle with four symbols inside, one for each element. The Master Shaper symbol. According to Lucian, it was the same symbol that adorned the powerful amulet he sought.

The Kessoku woman tossed the notebook to the man just as she looked over her shoulder. When she saw Talise's eyes on her, her eyes narrowed to a glare.

The woman pulled something with a shiny blade from her tunic, but Talise had already ducked before it could hit her.

By the time she looked back up, the man and woman had neared the archway that led out of the room.

Talise needed that amulet research. She needed the other notebook too. If it really contained Kessoku prison records, then it would have information about Wendy's brother, Cyrus. The battle in the room waged, but those notebooks would be worth any risk.

She glanced around for a quick assessment. Wendy stood in one corner with a palace soldier on either side of her. Loose strands flew from her braid, but her shaping was magnificent.

Wendy didn't need help.

Glancing behind her, Talise quickly determined Aaden also didn't need help. A little more sweat than usual slid down his hairline, but other than that, he looked is usual self.

Just as Talise decided to chase after the notebooks, far too many things happened all at once.

A shrill wail cut through the air. She identified it in an instant.

Tempest teetered on one foot while a line of blood slid down her opposite leg. She had a sword in one hand, but two Kessoku soldiers fought her at the same time. Even with her palace training, Tempest struggled against two at once.

The man with the notebooks neared the archway. If he got much further, Talise would lose sight of him completely.

Talise's gut pulled in two different directions. It felt just like her dream.

Master Shaper Talise would want her to help Tempest. Princess Talise would want her to go after the notebooks.

Too many allegiances fought for her attention. Was she a Master Shaper or was she the princess? Who needed her help the most?

She took one step toward Tempest, shooting a fire ball at the attackers. But then Talise took two steps back, anxious to keep an eye on the man with the notebooks.

Everything around her moved so fast, and it felt like she couldn't breathe. She just needed a moment. Just one second while she tried to decide.

A heavy silver vase swung down and suddenly the dilemma wisped away like an afterthought.

Aaden.

One of the Kessoku soldiers had slammed the vase onto Aaden's head, knocking him out. His body hung limp as the Kessoku threw him over his shoulder.

Before Talise could shout or attack or anything, the man ran toward the archway with Aaden on his back.

The noises of the room faded to the back of her mind. The movements around her blurred into indistinct forms. With perfect clarity, her mind focused in on the only thing that mattered.

She had to get Aaden back.

THIRTEEN

TALISE SPED OVER THE STONE FLOOR.

The cuts on her feet twisted and stung as she ran. The man carrying Aaden over his shoulder moved with impossible speed. He jumped over rocks and fallen bodies like they were tiny flowers in a meadow.

When he rounded a corner, something whispered at the back of her mind. *Be careful.* Where did that corridor lead?

But visions of sword-wielding Kessoku popping out from the corner weren't enough to slow her steps. If Kessoku wanted Aaden, there had to be a reason. Or a *person* who wanted him.

Her heart twisted when she remembered the moment she laid eyes on Lucian. She harbored an enormous amount of hate for that man. Every time she thought of him, she remembered when Aaden's voice broke in the treasury. He spoke of how his father had ruined his life.

But if he was given the chance, would he let his father repair their relationship? No matter how much bitterness he nurtured, could he really deny his own father?

None of that mattered. It didn't matter at all because she would rescue Aaden, and he never had to know about his father.

She rounded a corner just in time to see the Kessoku man disappear through a doorway. The wood dug into her palm as she slid the door open again. The man jumped at the sight of her, which sent Aaden to a crumpled mess on the floor.

Her heart caught in her throat when his head bounced on the stone. She didn't have time to worry. The Kessoku stood in front of her with his muscled arms at the ready.

"Get out!" the man shouted at her.

She attempted a smile. "Funny. I was about to say the same thing to you."

Apparently, he didn't care for comedy. The man balled his hands into fists. When the first one swung toward her, she let it swipe across her ear. The next hit, she took a careful step back so it would hit her in the stomach. But not too hard.

Just when the man took a confident step forward, she jammed her foot into his ankle. His arms flailed as he lost his balance. While he teetered, she slammed the side of her palm into the man's neck.

It wasn't perfect. He saw the hit coming and tilted his head away just enough that the blow didn't knock him out. But he did land hard on his backside. With his attention on dodging her blow, he did nothing to catch his fall.

The resulting hit on the stone floor caused the wind to knock out of him. He let out a few coughs, immediately following them with huge gulps of air.

Just when the man prepared to take another gulp, Talise shaped the air away from his mouth, leaving him even more oxygen starved than before. He clutched his throat and tried to take another breath.

Talise shaped the air away from him again, then delivered a more precise hit to his neck. This time, he lost consciousness.

Before his shoulder even hit stone, she had reached Aaden's side. His cheek jiggled as she patted it in quick bursts. "Wake up, wake up." Her voice felt stretched out and thin. "Please hurry, Aaden, I don't know how long he'll be out."

When he didn't move, she cradled his head in her lap and patted his cheeks even harder. "Aaden!" she said through a hiss.

Finally, his eyelids began fluttering. She let out a breath of relief as she ran her fingers through his hair.

"Well, this is a nice way to wake up," Aaden said, reaching for her face.

She held his hand against her cheek long enough to put on a smile. Then, she began to stand. "We have to get out of here. I don't know how long he'll stay unconscious."

Aaden followed her pointed finger over to the unconscious Kessoku. His eyebrows flew up to his forehead. "You knocked him out? By yourself?"

She was already hurrying toward the door as she nodded.

He grinned. "You're very impressive, do you know that?"

Heat crept into her neck and through her cheeks. "We need to go, Aaden. The fight is still going. They need our help." Her fingers curled as she gripped the hem of her tunic. "And I saw this notebook the Kessoku grabbed. Actually, there are two notebooks. One has information about Wendy's brother, and the other one..."

A knot of fear twisted inside her. But why? She had talked to Wendy about the amulet. Wendy knew even more than she did. So, why was she so hesitant to mention it to Aaden?

"We need to talk." Aaden had moved so close she could feel his breath ruffle her hair. How had he recovered so fast?

He looked afraid. Or possibly apprehensive. No, concerned. He looked concerned and that concerned her.

When he reached for her, his hands felt cold. Her eyes shot up to his, but they didn't speak to her the way they usually did.

She could only see how the skin wrinkled at the bottom corner of his eyes. It perfectly mirrored the almost frown he wore. Her heart skittered. It wasn't sure whether to speed up or stop altogether.

Just when Aaden opened his mouth again, the Kessoku let out a groan. Talise moved her hand into Aaden's grasp when he offered it. Before the man could stir again, they were already flying down the corridor hand in hand.

Talise pointed out the way back to the fight, but Aaden only shook his head. He led her down another corridor until a few empty rooms came into view. He chose the closest one and slid the door closed behind them.

Her palms felt clammy as she pulled away from his grasp. His lips had moved to form a tight line. His eyebrows knitted together.

Forget concerned, she was straight up scared now. She feared the silence, but she feared his words even more. "We have to get back to the fight," she said. "And I *need* those notebooks. We don't have time to talk."

Again, he ignored her insistence. He slid the door open a crack and glanced outside before he turned back to face her. Was he looking for someone?

Her heart decided to turn into a mallet, slamming against her chest.

"The emperor asked me to be a spy." He wouldn't look at her as he said the words. His eyes kept jumping to different corners of the room. He gulped.

Did he have to be so fidgety? Her fingers shook just from looking at him. She clasped them behind her back, desperate to regain some control. "What does that mean? He wants you to follow the Kessoku who leave this base? He wants you to sneak up on them as they travel?"

Aaden gulped again, which made her increasingly aware of the lump in her throat. His fingers ran over his normally neat hair, which sent at least four strands out of place. "He wants me to join them."

She blinked.

"To *pretend* to join them," he quickly amended.

When he reached for her, she took a step back. "No."

Thoughts went reeling inside her. A hundred and one versions of that story rushed through her mind and not one of them had a happy ending. "You can't do it. It's too dangerous. What if they find out you're lying? What if they trick you? What if they hurt you?"

Aaden sighed as he rested his forearm on the nearby wall. "I don't love the idea, but you have to admit, they're more likely to trust me than anyone else. The emperor wants me to do it today. He wants me to join the retreating Kessoku as soon as we gain control of the base."

His voice nearly broke as the words came out. His nose wrinkled as if his statement tasted like bile in his mouth.

"Don't do it. You *can't* do it. What if you start to believe..." Her voice trailed off before she said anything too incriminating, but it didn't matter.

The scar over Aaden's eye twitched as his eyebrows drew closer together. His eyes held pain. She could see how it affected him. He thought they were past this. So did she. But the truth hung between them as present as it had ever been.

She didn't trust him.

Her throat constricted when she tried to speak. She wanted to reach for him, but her arms seemed pinned at her sides. "Why did you look up my testing record?" she asked. "You found out I could shape all four elements when I was tested for the academy, but that's not what you wanted to know. What were you trying to find?"

He leaned into the wall as he let out a sigh. "Is this really the best time to ask me that?"

His words sliced through her gut. He wanted her to believe he had an innocent purpose, yet he gave no reason for her to believe otherwise. "Just tell me why." Her boots scraped the floor as she took a step forward. The reluctance in her voice had carried down to her toes. "Was it really because you wanted to know how someone from the Storm could shape?"

He gave her a single glance before staring back at the ground. His silence spoke more than words ever could. No. That wasn't the reason, and he wasn't going to tell her the real one.

She took a step back.

He reached out to her immediately. "I know you don't understand, but I have to do this. I have to be a spy."

"Why?" Tears started burning in the back of her throat. "You said the emperor *asked* you. So technically, it wasn't an order."

He curled his hand into a fist and pressed it against his forehead. "No, it wasn't an order, but I still have to do it."

She folded her arms across her chest. "What would happen if you don't? Did the emperor threaten to beat you again?"

The loose strands from Aaden's hair fluttered as he shook his head. "He didn't threaten..." His head cocked to the side. Suddenly, he stared into her eyes with a deeper intensity. "What do you mean *again*?"

A puff of air burst through her mouth as she tightened the muscles in her arms. "I know he beat you that day after you told him to stop yelling at me. You defied him, and then you left the training hall without being dismissed." She looked to the side, digging her nails into her arms as she spoke. "The next day your face was covered in bruises. You wouldn't explain what happened, but it wasn't hard to figure out."

"That wasn't the emperor." Aaden's voice came out flat. His jaw tight.

She let one hand wave through the air dismissively. "I don't mean him personally. I assumed he had one of his guards do the actual hitting. So he wouldn't injure his precious hands."

"No." Aaden stepped toward her. "It wasn't the emperor. He knew nothing about that until after it happened."

Talise narrowed her eyes. "Then who was it? How can you expect me to believe—"

"It was my grandfather."

Her eyes flew to his.

"He's the one who hit me."

Her limbs had frozen while the words trickled through her. His *grandfather*. Commander Blaise was the only person she had ever seen Aaden give unflinching respect to. But had that respect been earned from fists?

Aaden went back to the wall. He rested his forearm on the stone and pressed his forehead into his forearm. "The emperor told my grandfather what happened in the training hall and he..." An audible gulp sounded through the room. "He wanted me to remember it is unacceptable to defy the emperor."

Her voice was still frozen. Her feet were lead. But she managed to reach out and touch his hand.

"It's fine." His hand jerked away from her. "I don't need you to. ...I'm fine. I just didn't want you to think it was the emperor."

"Aaden." She wanted to talk, but what could she say? No words seemed adequate to heal the raw edges on her heart.

"Why don't you trust me?" An ache clung to his voice, but his eyes broke her. They were pleading. Hurting.

It pained her to see him like this. To know she contributed to his pain. So, she said the words that plagued her. It may have been a mistake, but when he looked at her like that, she could deny him nothing.

"Your father works for Kessoku."

A flash of fire went through his eyes. His head jerked as if shaking away an irritation. "No. He never worked for them. It wasn't like that. He—"

"I saw him."

Talise knew these words would surprise Aaden, but she didn't expect him wrap his arms around his stomach like he'd been punched in the gut. "What?"

Her fingers found the hem of her burlap tunic, and she stared down at it, unable to meet Aaden's eyes any longer. "He came to the dungeon. He questioned me." She pulled at the hem, forcing a thread loose just so she could pull it out. "The other Kessoku called him *general*."

"No." It was more an appeal than a statement. His fingers dug into his scalp, throwing his hair into complete disarray. Suddenly, his eyes shot up. "How do you know it was him? Maybe he just *said...*"

His voice trailed off when she shook her head. "You look just like him," she said under her breath.

She could practically feel his soul crushing as he pressed his forehead against the stone wall once more. She didn't want to hurt him any more, but she didn't have the luxury of time. The battle still waged in the other room and decisions needed to be made now.

"If you pretend to join Kessoku and your father is there, what would stop you from turning to their side? He's your father."

And your grandfather apparently likes to hit you is what she didn't add. She reached for him, desperate for contact. "No one could expect your allegiance to the crown to be stronger than your allegiance to family."

The moment she reached him, he wrapped his hand around her waist and pulled her a few steps closer. He used his other hand to stroke her cheek as he stared into her eyes. "Maybe my strongest allegiance isn't to the crown or to my family."

She turned her face away. "Don't say that, Aaden. Don't give me hope like that when there is so much at stake. He's your *father*."

Heat seeped into her back as Aaden's arm got warmer. "He left me."

"This is Kamdaria," she said with a sigh. "Family lasts forever."

His hand slid around her waist until it found her spine. Without stepping forward, he moved his body closer. He gulped. While tracing small circles into the small of her back, he asked. "If I do what the emperor asks and become a spy, you won't ever trust me?"

She buried her face in his chest, relieved when he brought his arms around her tight. "I want to trust you. You have no idea how much I want to. But he's your father, I can't ignore that. And... and they do have some compelling ideas, but their methods are all wrong. If you go, I'll spend every second wondering if you've already turned. I can't do that to myself. And it isn't fair to you either."

When she pulled away, he seemed to understand. At least his eyes looked subdued rather than angry. She took a step back, and a chill spread through her. "If you go, I can't keep doing this." She gestured at the air between them. "Whatever *this* is, I can't do it if you pretend to join Kessoku. No more kisses. No more private moments. It would be over."

His signature smirk graced his face as he reached back out to her. "But if I stay?"

She obliged without a thought, stepping into his embrace. The heat of his lips felt like fire in her mouth. But the kind of fire that warmed the heart, not the kind that blistered skin.

The door crashed open.

A fist came swinging toward them before Talise could get her bearings. The fist caught her in the jaw, swinging her head back.

Her skull jarred after the hit. When she blinked the stars out of her eyes, she recognized her attacker. The same man who had knocked out Aaden earlier.

He wasn't happy.

FOURTEEN

TALISE SENT HER OWN FIST AT THE Kessoku soldier attacking her. She jabbed and kicked with wild abandon, not focusing enough for targeted attacks. But how could she focus when Aaden just stood there?

His hands had flown twice as if to hit the soldier, but when it came time to do so, he simply blocked the blows instead.

Was he going to do it? Was he going to leave her and become a spy?

He glanced back at her while indecision colored his every feature. After a glance into her eyes, his jaw flexed. He lurched forward, barreling into the man's chest. He sent two hard blows to the man's head.

The man didn't lose consciousness, but he paused in pain long enough for Talise to jump past him toward the door.

Aaden caught her hand before they took off down the corridor. This holding-hands-while-running thing wasn't the most practical idea in the world, but deep down she needed it. For a moment, she truly believed Aaden would abandon her.

It felt nice to feel his presence at her side.

When they reached the archway leading to the strategy room, Talise's feet planted to the ground with an abrupt stop.

An empty room sat before them. The only people left were corpses.

"*There* you two are," Wendy said from down the corridor.

Talise whirled around to see her friend with a dagger in each hand. Wendy's flushed cheeks shimmered with sweat. Her hair looked more knotted mess than braid. A tear ripped through one side of her tunic, but no blood stained the fabric at least.

Talise glanced back at the empty room. "Is the fight over?"

"Not yet." Wendy jogged toward them, her breath coming in sharp pants. "Our reinforcements came a few minutes ago. Most of the Kessoku have retreated, but a few of them are still fighting. We pushed them out to the edges of the base."

Wendy tossed one of the daggers toward Talise.

"Thanks," Talise said when she caught it. She caught a glimpse of the flame-carved hilt and bit her lip. Slowly handing it toward Aaden, she said, "Actually, I guess this is yours."

He pushed it away, letting their hands touch a little longer than necessary. "Keep it. This isn't over yet. Where is everyone?"

Without a word, Wendy beckoned them as she ran down the corridor. They turned a few times. Talise lost the last sense of direction she had in those few turns. Everything seemed unfamiliar to her now. Dirt caked the stone in this part of the base. Debris littered the ground. Everything from broken chairs to smashed ink pots and even a soft blanket covered the floor.

After a few more turns, the noises of battle became clear. Weapons clashed, but they didn't seem as loud as earlier. Just before Wendy ducked through an archway, a shadow caught Talise's eye. She glanced back and noticed two figures tiptoeing down an opposite corridor.

Without a word to the others, Talise bolted after them. Their willowy figures made them easy to recognize. These were the same two Kessoku who had snatched those notebooks. They must have been looking for a way out of the base that didn't take them through the middle of a battle.

After a few steps, the Kessoku seemed to realize they had someone on their heels. Their speed increased. Talise urged herself to run faster, but the throbbing cuts on her feet protested.

When they disappeared through a doorway, Talise growled and forced herself to run harder.

Footsteps pounded from behind her. A moment later, Wendy appeared at her side, heaving as she brushed the hair away from her face. "I know they're Kessoku, but they don't even have weapons. Just let them go."

Talise shook her head, which disoriented her more than she expected. "They have information," she said through a pant. "Notebooks."

She couldn't manage anymore while running. Wendy nodded and pushed forward.

The Kessoku tried to escape through a doorway, but a wall of fire appeared in front of it. Since Talise hadn't done it herself, it had to have been Wendy or Aaden. It looked like Aaden's work.

At last, they reached the end of the corridor. The two Kessoku found themselves facing a wall. They each turned and backed into it as if eager to disappear inside.

"Give me the notebooks," Talise said through her teeth.

The two Kessoku glanced at each other with looks of horror.

"Both of them." Talise hoped she sounded authoritative. Did other leaders do that? Did they constantly worry if their voice held enough authority, or if they were even doing the right thing? Maybe someday she'd get used to the feeling.

When Talise stepped forward, panic seemed to ignite in the female Kessoku's eyes. "Do it," she said to her companion.

The man nodded and wrenched the two notebooks from his tunic.

Talise lunged, but she couldn't get there fast enough. While she moved toward him, he threw both notebooks into the air and shot each with a fire ball. Flames engulfed the pages inside before she had a second to breathe.

No.

It couldn't be too late yet. She just had to put out the fire. There had to be something salvageable inside. There *had* to be.

Talise's mind whirled while the notebooks fell. By the time they reached the ground, she had made her decision. They fell on opposite sides of the corridor, so she couldn't put them both out by herself.

She didn't choose the notebook that fell closest to her. Instead she lunged for the notebook with the gate embossed on the cover. The notebook with information about Cyrus. Using her body, she smothered the flame, hardly noticing or caring whether it burnt her clothes in the process.

"Save the other one," she shouted as she jumped.

In a flash, Wendy had jumped over the notebook that held the amulet research.

Amidst the chaos, the two Kessoku had run. Aaden went after them, but they had moved too fast for him.

Talise dropped herself on top of the notebook a few more times before she dared lift her body completely. When she did, the brown leather had been singed black. She sucked in a breath as she lifted the corner.

The edges of the paper were blackened, but most of it had survived. She let out a breath. Her heart throbbed as she gingerly turned page after page. All of them were safe.

The paper didn't look pretty. Some pages burned more than the others, but the information remained untainted.

After closing the notebook, she held it against her heart and let out a long breath. The pulsing in her veins nearly stopped as she turned around.

Wendy held her hands outstretched, the notebook with the amulet research perched on top. She bit her lip, staring intensely, as if too afraid to open it.

Talise nodded, urging her friend to act.

Wendy reached for a small bit of hair and twirled it once before she finally grabbed the corner of the notebook. When she opened it, the pages inside crumbled to ash. Her eyebrows flew up her forehead as she forced the notebook open even wider. She looked eager to find even one page that had survived.

But not one had.

Ash fluttered to the ground in blackened heaps.

"I wasn't fast enough." Wendy's head hung with the words.

It hurt. They had needed that notebook too. But Talise merely pulled the other notebook closer to her chest. "It's okay." She had made her decision, and for once, she didn't question it.

Aaden came down the corridor toward them with heavy steps. "I lost them," he said in a dark voice.

Talise tucked the notebook into her burlap tunic as she stood. "It's okay," she said again. When she started back down the corridor, the others followed without a word. Just before rounding the corner, someone rushed around it, slamming into Talise.

The collision caused her to take several steps backward.

The person's hair flew out in a wave around her face as she fell backward. When she landed on the ground, Talise finally recognized her.

Tempest scrambled to her feet and grabbed Talise by the shoulders. "Master Shaper Talise." She rested her head in her hands as she let out a big sigh. "Oh, I'm so glad to see you. I thought you were dead." She flicked Aaden in the arm. "Aaden would have killed me." Her hand flew upward as if reaching for the ceiling. "The emperor would have killed me." She glanced to Talise's side. "*Wendy* would have killed me."

"Where is everyone?" Talise asked.

Tempest waved her hand through the air. "Oh, all over. We seized the base. All the Kessoku have been killed, been taken prisoner, or they've escaped. A group of them are retreating now, probably to their base in the Gate."

Aaden twitched at these words, but he didn't move. Apparently, his decision was final too.

Wendy continued, "Then, some of the army will stay here to maintain control, but it's time for the rest of us to go home."

Home.

For the first time in three weeks, Talise could breathe.

FIFTEEN

ON HER WAY UP TO THE PALACE doors, Talise couldn't help thinking of six months earlier when she had arrived for the competition.

Aaden had hated her then. He might have already been planning a way to sabotage her demonstration. Wendy and Claye had been whispering hurriedly, both anxious to find out if their demonstrations would be enough to get them jobs inside the palace.

Things seemed simpler back then. Their lives hadn't yet been tainted by the recent attacks. Talise hadn't been broken by the difficulty of the trials. She and Aaden were still enemies.

The past six months since the competition had been anything but easy, but Talise found gratitude for every moment of them. They shaped her into someone new. Someone better. She poked her tunic, feeling through it for the notebook inside.

At last she knew who she really was.

A set of guards trailed both in front and behind Talise. Supposedly, her true identity remained secret, but being guarded this heavily everywhere she went was bound to make people suspicious.

For now though, hopefully everyone would assume her Master Shaper status afforded her the extra protection.

Even the smell of the palace felt familiar as she walked through the doors. With autumn approaching, the cherry trees had long since lost their blossoms. But the cedar walls and beams gave off a familiar scent. And the usual dinner smells of ginger and soy wafted through the air.

To her surprise, the guards didn't lead them toward the throne room. Instead, she noticed a long line of people spilling out of the throne room doors. Many of them wore scowls, and at least half had their arms crossed over their chests.

The guards took them around a few corners until they reached the hallway leading to her own living quarters. The guards left then, allowing her mind more room to think. Before she could wonder at the line of people coming from the throne room, a friendly voice came from behind her.

"You're alive." A beaming smile covered Claye's face. He nearly knocked Talise over with the force of his hug. "We received word yesterday, but I was afraid to believe it."

His presence brought her a surprising amount of comfort.

"Of course she's alive," Wendy said wearing an even bigger smile. "We'd never let her rot in some stupid dungeon."

Claye took a step back and tapped his chin as he looked Talise over from head to toe. The whole thing made her feel like a child whose parent was trying to decide if she was ready for school.

"You don't look too underfed," Claye said, still tapping his chin. Suddenly, he stopped and pointed. "What happened to your hand?"

Talise let out an embarrassed smile as she lifted her gauze covered fingers. "Frostbite."

He mouthed the word before he let out a laugh. "Well, at least we know you aren't invincible." He laughed again and pulled her in for another hug. A minty smell clung to his clothes.

"We missed you," he said in her ear before pulling away.

The moment he stepped away, Aaden reached for her hand, lacing their fingers together.

A smile grew on Claye's face when he saw their hands. He leaned forward. "Aaden's the one who found you. Did he tell you that?"

At her side, Aaden shuffled one foot across the ground. He wouldn't look her way, but the hint of a smile lingered on his lips. That didn't surprise her. Aaden never bragged.

Claye bobbed his head up and down. "Yep. After you were taken, he stayed up for two days straight trying to find you. The emperor finally had to order him to get some sleep. Aaden was..." Claye tapped his fingers together under his chin. "How do I put this lightly?"

"Not happy?" Wendy suggested.

Claye let out a snort. "Ready to murder everyone who kidnapped you is probably more accurate, but yeah, let's go with *not happy.*"

When Aaden pulled her closer, she went without hesitation. "Let's go. I'm sure the emperor wants you back in your living quarters." He looked over his shoulder, his eyes narrowing at the sounds coming from the rest of the palace.

Once they were on their way, Talise asked, "Who were all those people in the throne room? Why were they in a line?"

Aaden, Wendy, and Claye all glanced at each other while silence hung in the air. Aaden gulped. Wendy twirled a piece of her hair.

"Yeah," Claye said, elongating the syllable for several seconds. "Remember how Kessoku attacked and killed the Master Shapers and a bunch of other people, and the emperor decided not to tell anyone? And remember how Kessoku attacked at the masquerade ball in front of a bunch of citizens?" He shrugged. "Now everyone knows about the attacks. All of them."

Talise blinked.

"The people are angry," Aaden said. "They're mad the emperor lied to them."

Wendy clasped her hands in front of her chest. "We're doing damage control, but..." She pursed her lips as she looked to the side. "It's going to be awhile before the emperor gains their trust back."

When they arrived at Talise's rooms, she shoved everyone inside. She pushed Aaden and Claye over to the two chairs at her breakfast table, then sent Wendy to the chair in front of the desk.

As she pulled the notebook from her tunic, she made a mental note to get two more chairs for her breakfast table. "I heard two Kessoku talking when they found this notebook." Her voice lowered, leaning even closer to her friends. "It contains prison records." Her eyes turned to Wendy. "Kessoku's prisoners."

Claye seemed to just manage to suppress his eye roll, but he didn't drain all the sarcasm from his voice. "How *exciting*."

"Cyrus." Wendy's voice came out as a whisper. Claye's sarcasm had been forgotten. Even Aaden leaned closer to the notebook.

Talise nodded. "We need to give the notebook to the emperor. If it has information about the prisoners, it could also have information about their bases and possibly leadership, that sort of thing." Talise gulped as she handed the notebook out to her friend. "But I thought you should get a chance to look at it first."

Wendy took the notebook solemnly. Her eyes showed real hope for the first time in a long time. With the leather in the hands of her friend, Talise knew she had made the right choice saving that notebook and not the other.

Now they could know once and for all if Cyrus was alive.

SIXTEEN

THE WOOL CAPE AROUND TALISE'S shoulders fought the chill of the outside air.

She hadn't visited the palace graveyard at all since she won the competition. Her last time seeing it had been through the gate that separated the graveyard from the grounds of the elite academy.

But tonight, death was on her mind. So many prisoners had died. So many had been tortured and killed without reason. Without cause.

But not all of them.

Cyrus was still alive. The news had been enough to make everyone cry. Wendy had skipped around Talise's living quarters with joyful tears streaming down her face. After a few minutes of that, she had pulled them all into a group hug and even Aaden cracked a smile.

The day got even better when they had given the notebook to the emperor and discovered it named all of Kessoku's bases and even gave vague location details for a few of them. New plans had been made in a matter of hours.

They were going to find Kessoku's bases in the Gate and seize control of all of them. If things went according to plan, their enemy might be beaten by Water Festival in mid-winter.

Talise hugged the cape tighter around her shoulders.

But not all the prisoners had survived. As joyous as the day had been, a wedge had driven itself into Talise's heart when she remembered the first casualties of this war.

At last, she found the gravestone that had prompted so many of her tears. Kneeling in front of the stone, Talise read her mother's name.

Isla Tempest Malksur Ruemon

Empress of Kamdaria

Over a thousand marks adorned the grave, but Talise traced her finger over the mark carved just under the *I*.

Talise had made that mark. As a five-year-old, her shaping hadn't been advanced enough to leave a proper mark. But Marmie had helped her use a mallet and chisel to carve in a small mark. It had been night then too.

She and Marmie had left their marks in the dead of night before they ran to hide in the most unlikely place of all. The Storm.

Talise leaned her head against the stone and reached for her heart just as it seemed to splinter into pieces. She and Marmie had risked getting caught just so they could leave a mark on the graves of their family.

The marks on her brothers' and sisters' graves had been left in a hurry, but Talise had still marked them because this was Kamdaria, and family lasted forever. Even in death.

Her throat ached. Her stomach churned. The tears fell as the memory of her risks took hold. She'd been able to risk her life for the graves of her mother and her brothers and sisters, but not for Marmie.

She had made her peace with that. Or tried to anyway. But sitting in the graveyard, the pain cut through her as she imagined Marmie's grave sitting bare in the Storm. Not a single mark to honor it.

Talise swiped her wrist across her nose before she pulled a worn letter from her cloak. No matter how bare Marmie's gravestone was, Talise was still determined her sacrifice would never be forgotten.

Though technically her aunt, Marmie had become a second mother to Talise even before the Kessoku's attack. She had always been there when Talise needed her. Even in her dream at the Kessoku base.

The letter crinkled as Talise smoothed it out. She read the words that had helped her so many times.

Without hope, people have nothing. They aren't happy; they don't live. But the smallest things can change that.

Marmie had been talking about the flower she finally got growing in the Storm, but the words held so much more meaning to Talise now. Just like in her dream, Talise knew people from the Storm were dangerous and frightening. But they only needed hope, and that could change everything.

She still had to find out more about the amulet, and they still had to stop Kessoku and seize their bases. They had to find and rescue Cyrus. But more than ever, Talise knew she had more than that to do.

She would save the Storm.

In Kessoku's base, so much turmoil plagued her while she tried to decide if her role as Master Shaper or as princess was more important. She wondered if the soldiers needed her more or if the emperor did.

The notebook had changed everything. As Master Shaper, she would have let the notebooks go and focused on seizing the base. As princess, she would have saved the amulet research to ensure the emperor had everything he needed to fight his enemy.

But she had chosen something else entirely. She chose Kamdaria. The people of Kamdaria needed to know what had happened to their family members. Now, thanks to the prison records, they would be able to find out.

Clasping the letter tight in her hand, she lifted her eyes to the sky. Whispering, she spoke to the air. "You died for me, Marmie. I promise I won't let your life be lost in vain."

Talise took in a breath, squeezing the letter against her heart. "Of all the titles, I've held in my life, I finally realized which is the most important. From now on, I'm not just the princess or a Master Shaper. I will be Defender of Kamdaria."

Tears slid down her cheeks as she finished. Her throat seared from the ache. After touching her mark in her mother's grave once more, she took a few minutes in front of the other graves. She touched her mark on each grave and thought of their lives. Honored them.

When she had finished, her heart felt both full and empty all at the same time. They were gone now, but she would make things right.

While tucking the letter back into her cloak, the sound of crunching gravel made her freeze. She looked into the night for whoever had found her. Perhaps one of the emperor's guards had noticed she snuck out of bed.

A tall figure wore a cloak over their head making the face unrecognizable. But the figure didn't seem to be there for her at all. Whoever it was moved swiftly past the graveyard toward the boats that led to the Gate.

She followed without thought. When her own footsteps began crunching over the gravel, the hidden figure turned. For a moment, the light of the palace spilled onto his face. Even after he hastily dropped his head, so the hood would hide him, it didn't matter. She had already seen.

Aaden.

She clutched her chest while her throat swelled. Was it possible for her heart to break any more? Apparently, it was.

She glanced down at the boats and then back to Aaden. He turned away with his shoulders hunched, as if trying to make himself look smaller.

The boats took people to the Gate. The Gate only had one thing he would want.

Kessoku.

With her throat so tight, she had to squeeze her voice through. "I thought you weren't going to go."

He had the decency to look her in the eye. He pulled his hood back just enough that she could see how pain traced over his features. "I wasn't going to but..." His voice seemed even tighter than hers. He stared with longing in his eyes before he looked down. He dropped his head into his hand. "He's my *father*."

The patter of her heart sent a flurry of terror through her entire body. "Please don't go."

His lip trembled before he whirled around. "I have to." His fists tightened at his side as he began stepping faster than before. When she followed after him, he flicked his hand as if shooing her away. "I'll report back in two weeks. If I'm not back by then, you have every right to distrust me."

"Aaden." Her feet had frozen in place with her arms outstretched. But he didn't see. He marched forward without a single glance back.

The tightness in her throat hardened. Her fingers formed fists. "Don't you dare leave me like this. I swear on Kamdaria, if you leave right now, I'll never forgive you."

His steps didn't waver.

"I mean it!" Her voice cracked as she spoke, but they had no effect on his retreating figure.

"Aaden." A single word had never conveyed her heartbreak so completely than in this moment.

At last, he turned. The hood shielded his face, leaving only his lips and goatee visible. The stillness lasted long enough to fill her bones with ice. When he spoke, the words ate her from the inside out.

"I'll miss you," he said.

And then he was gone. Her knees hit the gravel while his betrayal punched hole after hole into her shattered heart.

She had so much to do. So much to change.

But how could she defend Kamdaria with a heart broken in two?

FIND OUT WHAT HAPPENS NEXT!

Talise's story continues in River Gate, The Elements of Kamdaria 5.

The people of Kamdaria are angry. Talise must gain back their loyalty before its lost forever.

DEAR READER,

Thank you so much for reading my book! If you liked it, please consider leaving a review on amazon or goodreads. Reviews are so helpful to me as an author, plus they help other readers know if a book is right for them.

To receive special offers, bonus content, and info on my new releases and other great reads, sign up for my email list! Psst, you'll get my short story collection for FREE. :)

www.KayLMoody.com/gift

Printed in Great Britain
by Amazon

43462985R00095